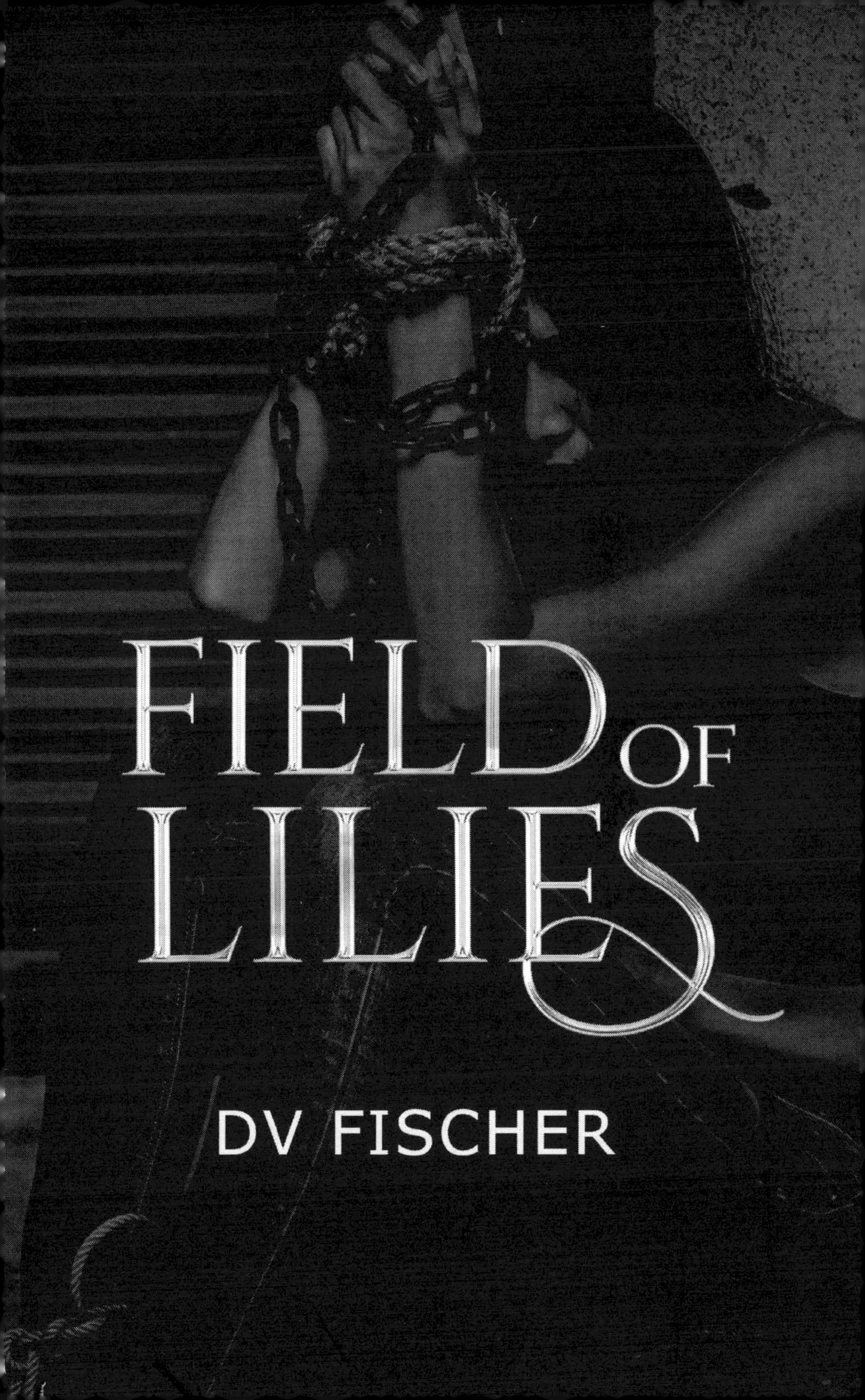
FIELD OF LILIES
DV FISCHER

FIELD OF LILIES

A Curvy Girl Dark Romance

DV FISCHER

Field of Lilies (A Curvy Girl Dark Romance)

Editor: Dawn Yacovetta

Cover Designer: Artscandare Book Cover Design

ISBN Paperback: 979-8-9902675-4-1

ISBN Hardcover: 979-8-9902675-5-8

Follow DV Fischer

Follow DV Fischer on Facebook, Instagram, Amazon, Tiktok, Goodreads, and Bookbub.

HEAD TO MY WEBSITE FOR OTHER BOOKS AND BOOK WARNING TRIGGERS.

www.dvfischer.com

Playlist

Civil Wars by Devil's Backbone
I Walk the Line by Halsey
Save Yourself by Kaleo
Riverside by Agnes Obel
Blood On My Name by The Brothers Bright
The Way That I Feel by Danielle Parente

"If your flavor is vanilla, you came to the wrong ice cream shop."
Your Walking Red Flag, Killian Savage

Chapter 1

Tori Townsend

MY WINDSHIELD WIPERS SWIPE FRANTICALLY across the front window of my car. The rain pounds against the glass. Coupled with the dark night, the torrential downpour makes it hard to see the road in front of me.

My car doesn't miss the potholes, however. It can see just fine because it hits every single one like it's some sort of game. I swear, if one of my tires pops . . .

The last thing I want is to be out in this rain, changing a tire. Hell, I don't even know how to change a tire. Narrowing my eyes, I realize that I don't even know where the spare is.

Spring came in full swing two months ago for Fairview, Utah, and the rain has yet to let up despite the climbing temperatures and the blooming flowers. I'd almost prefer the snow if it weren't for the frigid wind that would come with it. It would be less likely that the bottom of my jeans would be as soaked as they currently are. I hate how they stick to my ankles, making them itchy.

The other week, I had caved and bought rain boots from

Derek Wordon's thrift store. Fashion sacrifices and all that. If only I had worn them today, but nothing screams professional about wearing rain boots to a house showing.

The boots aren't the only fashion sacrifice I'll have to make. I yank my shirt down over a rounder stomach that I didn't have a year ago and clench my jaw in irritation. The weight is forcing me to change my wardrobe and buy new clothes that fit me better, but I'm rebelling against it by telling myself I'll find time to work out. That I'll make room for returning my body to what it once was.

It's all a lie, and deep down, I know it.

Truth be told, my weight is because of my schedule. I used to pack lunches – carrots, celery, and salads. I used to be so good about what I ate, but now what I consume consists of convenience. A whole lot of junk food, pizza from Mount Pleasant, and frozen meals. And if I'm being honest, which I really don't want to be right now, I've been eating my feelings.

My life is stressful. Tegan tells me that two businesses are one too many for one person to handle. She's probably right, but I refuse to give up on my Wiccan shop *and* my realtor business, even if one is doing better than the other.

My tires dip into a particularly nasty pothole, and my phone, which had been resting on the dashboard, bounces, flies off, and lands on the floor by my feet.

"Fuck!" I hiss.

I bite my bottom lip as I consider what to do, flicking my eyes between what I can see of the road and my phone on the car's floor. Normally, I'd leave it, but the floor is soaked from my shoes and jeans. That could destroy the phone, and I need my phone for my businesses. That fact alone is enough to convince me to take action.

Carefully balancing the steering wheel with one hand, I reach blindly down to the floor with the other. My fingertips don't touch it right away, and I curse under my breath as I shift my eyes from the road down to the wet carpet.

Finally, my fingers graze it, and I snatch up the phone and blow out a breath as I right myself, throw it back on the dashboard, and return my eyes to the road.

Just ahead and parked on the side of the road is a black van with its blinkers on. I swerve a little to give them space, but my next breath is stolen from me.

I don't have time to brake.

I don't have time to scream.

A figure starts to dash across the road, and it takes a mere second for me and the woman's eyes to connect. My lights reflect across the pale skin of her frightened face and then . . .

I squeeze my eyes shut at the same time as I hit her with my car. As I slam on the breaks, I know then and there that I'll never forget the sound of her body hitting the hood of my car. The sickening thud. The crunch of glass.

The tires squeal to a stop, and I open my eyes, wildly searching what's in front of me. "Oh god. Oh god!"

There, lying twisted, rain pounding against her, is a woman sprawled out on the road.

I take one heavy breath. And then another.

"Oh god!" I sob-scream as the realization of what I've done slams into me like a ton of bricks.

Yanking open my door, I leave it ajar as I dash to her side and drop to my knees beside her. My hands hover an inch as they pass over her body, not knowing what to touch or what to do.

Dark, soaked hair sticks to her bloodied, high cheekbones, and wide, almond-shaped blue eyes stare off into the distance, toward the field of lilies that I can barely make out. Her ragged, frilly dress sticks to her body, pronouncing her swollen belly. A very pregnant belly.

I hit a pregnant woman.

Her leg is twisted the wrong way, and her arm is bent behind her. She doesn't move. She doesn't speak. I don't even think she can.

"You came out of nowhere," I cry out as I watch her struggle for breath. "Tell me what to do. Tell me what to do!"

Something in my peripheral vision catches my attention, and my head swivels in that direction. There, standing in the dark, is a figure. For the height, I assume it's a man. I squint against the rain running into my eyes. Because the hood is up, I can't make out his face, but his bright orange raincoat stands out against the darkness.

"Please!" I beg the man. "Help her!"

At the sound of my voice, the man turns and takes off in the direction he came from. I watch in horror as he sprints toward the driver's side of the black van, and I plead for his aid when he hops inside and peels away, passing us by at an accelerated speed. From his tires, water splashes over us, and I quickly lean over the woman to keep the majority of it off of her. I gasp as the giant puddle he ran through batters against my back.

Underneath me, the woman's breathing becomes more labored, more struggled.

I lean back a little and tip her head so she can look at me instead of off into the darkness. "I'm going to get help," I sob to her. "Please, please don't die. Help is coming. Okay? Keep breathing!"

She doesn't respond. She doesn't even blink as the rain pelts her open eyes and mixes with the blood dripping from her nose and mouth.

I scramble to my feet and race back to my car. As soon as I have my phone in my hand, I quickly swipe in the password and dial 9-1-1 while I jog back to the woman. I kneel down beside her as the line picks up, and before the man can spit out his formal greeting, I spew my emergency.

"Please! I hit a woman with my car!"

There's a pause on the line before he says, "Ma'am, where are you?"

"Next to the field of lilies!" I rattle off the road I'm on, and her chest stops rising. For a second, I hold my breath and wait for her lungs to fill, but they never do. "Oh god, she stopped breathing! What do I do? Tell me what to do!"

He pauses again, and it makes me want to scream. "Ma'am, help is on the way."

"Help is too late!" I yell into the phone, and then I end the call with a furious press of my finger.

"Oh god," I whisper over and over again. I tap her cheek as tears flow freely down my cheeks. "Please don't die. Please!" But it's no use.

Her eyes are unseeing.

Her chest is not moving.

The only sound is the rain pelting ominously around us, *around me*, because I'm alone with a woman I killed.

I lift my hands and sob into my palms.

Chapter 2

Tori Townsend

PEOPLE WALK AROUND ME, snapping pictures and chatting softly. The lights of the emergency vehicles flash against the wet pavement, and the rain continues to pound against my back.

They took her off the road some time ago, the whispering EMTs, but I can't bring myself to get off my knees. My mind keeps replaying the scene, reliving what I'd done. I've long since stopped crying, and my emotions have taken on this numb quality that I have never experienced before. I can feel that my life has shifted now that I've ended a life. It's almost as if I don't recognize myself. Like I'm wrapped in someone else's skin because this can't really be my life, can it?

I'm soaked and vaguely aware that I'm shivering so hard my entire body quakes and aches. Only when a blanket is laid over my shoulders do I look up from the outline of the lily field.

Dark eyebrows are pulled together as a familiar face peers down at me. Pierce Hilton opens his mouth to say something, but he must think better of it because he closes it, and his lips thin into a fine line. His brown eyes soften as they take in my expression, whatever that may be, and he bends his tall frame at the knees until he's squatting next to me. He may not be in his uniform, probably because it's the middle of the night, but he's still the new sheriff. His badge, pinned at the waist, flashes the ambulance lights back at me.

He's a handsome man. I've thought that since the day he moved here from New York with his grandfather. Even though his hair is dripping wet, it's tousled in a messy way, and his sweater clings to his slight build as it soaks from the rain.

Tucking the blanket tighter around my shoulders, he asks, "How are you holding up?"

I blink at him and then stare back at the pavement. I don't know how to answer that. I don't even know what this lack of feeling is.

"That bad, huh?" he murmurs over the noise surrounding us.

He reaches to push wet hair from my dripping face, but I veer my head away from his fingers. The almost-touch was too much, and I know damn well that he knows that too. We may have slept together once, but that doesn't make me his girl. Sometimes, he forgets that, and even though I'm vulnerable, my mind hasn't changed about exploring what he deems could be 'something good.'

"Don't," I murmur the warning gently.

He doesn't verbally give it away, but I can tell he's disappointed by the way he drops his hand onto his bent knee. "Sorry." The abrupt clearing of his throat makes me jump a bit. He glances around us and says, "We should get you somewhere warm though. At the very least, somewhere dry."

"I'm fine," I lie. My knees hurt from digging into the road, my neck aches from shivering, and the tip of my nose feels like it's an icicle. But I deserve this. *I deserve more than this.*

Giving a small shake of his head, he adds, "You can't stay here, Tori."

I turn a glare in his direction. I know he's just trying to help, but I don't want it.

He sighs. "Is there someone I can call for you?" He glances down at his shoes. "A boyfriend or something?"

I know he's fishing. Ever since we slept together, he's been trying to date me. I haven't directly told him no, but I thought my avoiding him was answer enough. At some point, I'll have to be straight with him. Right now isn't a good time, though, so I just shake my head.

"What about Tegan?" he mutters softly. "Do you want her?"

Taking a deep breath, I nod. My best friend is exactly who I need. Even though she's never murdered someone, she'll know precisely what to say and what to do. She's the only person I have.

He flags down an officer and tells him to call Tegan Garner, formerly Adams, to pick me up, and once that officer heads to his car to do just that, he turns back to me. Slowly, he stands and holds out his hand. I stare at the lines on his palm for a moment, and he waits patiently while I make a decision. I know he'll eventually pick me up if I don't move, so I choose the lesser of two evils and take his hand.

After he hauls me up, he readjusts my blanket and leads me to an empty ambulance. He angles his body just right so that I don't stare at the dead woman in the ambulance next to it. She may be in a black bag, but he's still trying to shelter me from the evidence anyway.

His grandfather is inside that ambulance, and I can hear him praying over the woman, asking God to take her soul and forgive her sins. Pierce's grandfather is the new pastor of one of Fairview's churches. I met him shortly after he moved here, and to say we don't get along is an understatement.

Pierce guides me to sit on the end of the ambulance and

out of the rain. Hopping up, he rummages around inside the ambulance's drawers, pulls out a fresh blanket, and takes off my soaked one. As soon as the new one is adjusted on my shoulders, he sits down next to me. His weight jostles the entire ambulance as he does so.

He blows out a breath, and then he looks at the side of my face. "I'm sorry, Tori, but I have to ask what happened."

I swallow thickly as the emotions threaten to rise, looking down at my pruney fingers. "She came out of nowhere."

"Where did she come from?" he presses gently.

My shrug is small as I begin pulling at my knuckles. "From a black van, I guess. It was on the side of the road. Had its lights flashing."

From the side of my vision, I can see him frown. "Did she just step out onto the road at the wrong time?"

I'm sure my scowl matches his own as I recount the event. "No, she was running. And she looked . . ." I swallow and curl my fingers into fists. "Afraid."

It doesn't take a genius to know that he's fidgeting because he wants to take my hand into his. Thankfully, he doesn't. Instead, he says, "There's no van here now, and the rain long since washed away the tracks. What happened to it?"

I slowly turn my head to look at him, wondering if he thinks that I'm making it up. However, I don't see that etched in the concerned lines on his face, so I explain. "The man in the orange raincoat took off with it when he'd seen what I'd done."

He nods a little and pulls out his phone. In a few taps, he brings up the notes app and asks, "What did this man look like?"

"I don't know. I couldn't see his face. The hood was pulled up, and with the darkness and the rain . . . He was tall. That's all I know."

His fingers fly across the screen of his phone as he jots

down what little I could give him. "And the van? Did you see the plates? Any unique details about it?"

I shake my head. "No. I-It-It was dark."

He glances over at me, and I can tell he's a bit frustrated by the slow drooping of his shoulders. "Was it a minivan?"

I shake my head again. "A big one." Fingers fly across the screen as he jots that down too. I turn my attention back to my cold hands. "I'm sorry. I don't have anything else. That really is all I know."

He's quiet for a moment before he pockets his phone. "Tegan should be here soon, and I want you to go home and take a warm bath."

I look at his chest. "Do you – The woman . . ."

"No, we don't know who she is. She had no identification, but we'll figure it out. I'll make sure I tell you as soon as I do, okay?"

"Okay," I whisper. I don't know what I'll do with that information, but at least, I'll know the name of the woman I hit. *Killed.* Maybe even learn her baby's name – or what it was supposed to be anyway.

I glance over to thank him for his kindness but suck in a breath as soon as an orange raincoat heads our direction.

"What?" Pierce asks, looking with me.

"That's the orange coat," I breathe. "The one the guy was wearing."

He scowls. "It's just my grandfather, Tori. And besides, everyone has that coat. Derek Wordon got a shipment of them for his store, and because of how much rain we've been getting, several people have bought them. They're all over town."

Oh. I guess I hadn't noticed.

The pastor, Kent Hilton, pulls down the hood of the raincoat and stares right at me. Glares is more like it. I glare right back because, well . . . I hate him. His belly extends and presses into the zipper, but otherwise, he's a thin man. White hair peppers his face, and a full head of it covers his scalp. For a man in his seventies, I'm surprised he isn't bald. His god must have blessed him, though I can't think why anyone would bless this man. He's an asshole.

"I should have known it was you," he grinds out.

I can't hide my flinch, but it's Pierce who comes to my aid. Normally, I'd have no problem sticking up for myself when it comes to this guy, but in my vulnerable state, it whips me speechless. "Don't start, Pap. Now isn't the time."

My nose wants to wrinkle in disgust. I never liked what he calls his grandfather. Even though he raised Pierce, he doesn't deserve endearments. Surely, Pierce can see his grandfather for what he truly is.

Kent points at me with a bony finger. "She's pagan."

"So, because she doesn't believe in God, she deserves this?" Pierce raises his eyebrows at the old man.

Dropping his hand back to his side, Kent only huffs.

"People who believe in God have this sort of thing happen to them all the time," Pierce presses on. "It's just shit luck. Nothing more."

"She's no good for a town like this," Kent growls. He sweeps out his arms to display the entire scene. "Look at the mess she created."

I pinch my eyebrows together and spit, "I lived here way before you came along, and everything was just fine."

Pierce hops off the ambulance, stands between us, and holds out his hands. He acts as if, at any moment, the argument will come to blows. "Look, I know you guys don't like each other, but now isn't the time."

The asshole glares at me from over his grandson's shoulder, and I glare right back. We do that a lot. He may be the old-school new pastor, but that's not his only occupation. Before he moved here, I was the only realtor in the area. As a side-gig, and as someone who saw an opportunity, he opened his own realtor business to compete against mine. And wouldn't you know it? His realtor office is right beside my Wiccan shop in Mount Pleasant.

He makes no bones about telling me or, shit, even showing me how me and my store don't belong here. He's making it hard to keep my shop open, spreading his hatred as he is.

Every time I see his face, I want to punch it.

"Tori?" I hear Tegan call. From wherever she is, I hear panic in her tone. "Where is she? Do you see her?" A second later, she's rounding the ambulances, dressed in only cat-patterned pajamas. As soon as she sees me, her shoulders relax, and she rushes in my direction.

Pierce steers his grandfather away, and I brace myself as Tegan comes barreling at me, arms wide open. She nearly knocks me down as she wraps her arms tightly around me.

Over her shoulder, I see Cole examining the damage to my car with a pinched expression. For a second, he glances at the body bag in the ambulance and then turns his gaze at me. His eyes soften for a moment, watching as his wife embraces me, and as he heads my direction, I squeeze my eyes shut to force the tears to stay tucked deep, deep inside me. To have two caring friends like them is more than anyone deserves.

"The officer told me what happened," Tegan says into my ear. I can hear the emotion in her tone, and I give her a squeeze before letting her go.

"Yeah," I whisper.

"Are you alright?" Cole asks as soon as he reaches us. He stuffs his hands into his coat pockets, and I note, like Tegan, he's also wearing pajamas.

I nod because I can't trust my voice. Emotionally, that's a lie. I'm not alright. But physically, I'm unharmed, which I think is what he's asking for.

"Your car is totaled," Cole grunts. "We'll get you a loaner car."

"I don't know where to get one of those," I confess.

"Derek has a few," he answers. He'd know as he pretty

much manages all of Derek's things. Mostly his rentals, but sometimes Derek throws more his way.

"Thank you," I mutter to him.

Tegan takes my wet face into her palms and forces me to look at her. I don't know what she sees in my eyes, but they cause hers to water. It takes everything I have not to cry with her. "Let's get you home."

Not trusting my voice, I nod.

Chapter 3

Killian Savage

WELCOME TO FAIRVIEW.

I stare at the aged stone sign as I stand on the side of the rough road with my backpack slung over my right shoulder. I don't need to be 'welcomed.' I just need a place to sleep for a few days.

My backpack strap starts to slip, so I readjust its position, wipe a hand over my tired eyes, and face forward. Through the haze, I can see the town – short squatting buildings in the center and townhomes dotted around it. And in the background, great hills and small mountains lift toward the gray, puffy clouds. Their surface is layered with bright green trees that sway in the wind.

It may be dawn, it may be sprinkling, and it may be small, but there it is. My destination. A far cry from New York, New York. I suppose my entire life is a far cry from the one I led back in the big city . . . Before everything changed.

My foot crunches on the gravel that's sprawled out on the shoulder of the road as I move forward. I hadn't walked here from the city. I took a few buses, but mostly, I hitchhiked. You'd be surprised how many people pull over for a drifter.

My last ride ended in Mount Pleasant, and I walked the rest of the way overnight. I could have easily stayed there, found a place to sleep like I normally do, but for some odd reason, Fairview is where I wanted to be.

I pull out my burner phone from my back pocket and swipe my finger around the screen to get through the password. It takes a second for me to pull up the browser. I'd done my research. Population under two thousand. They have a popular bakery, hiking trails, cabins, and fishing. Aside from the murder that happened last year, Fairview is a quiet town surrounded by peace. Or so it seems. Because every town has its secrets. It doesn't matter. I have every intention of staying for just a few days before I wander off again. My purpose isn't to live here because I won't rest until I find *him.* But even I have to admit that the small reprieve Fairview might offer is appealing.

I'm tired. Tired of wandering, tired of no answers, and tired of looking for a ghost, but I know he exists. I've lain eyes on him, broke his fingers and tore off his toenails, and watched him bleed from the deep gashes I gave him on his face. I heard him scream. And as soon as I let him go, he stole everything from me for what I'd done.

Often, I daydream about how I'll make him pay. Often, my fantasies get wild, but I have time to sort out every detail.

I pocket my phone when I reach the first townhouse. It may still be morning, but people are already awake and stretching their legs. An old lady walks her small dog along the sidewalk, eyeing me with curiosity. Her gaze rakes down my body, from my long hair tied back in a bun to my beaten leather jacket, and down to my tattooed hands. She pauses there but just for a second before coming to a conclusion and scurrying off with her dog.

She's not the only person who stares as I make my way

toward the center of town. I pass cars with people who crane their necks to get a good look and window peepers who snap the curtain shut as soon as I look them square in the eye.

I get it. I'm a stranger, and I don't look friendly, but I make it a habit to not pretend to be someone I'm not.

Take me as I am, or leave me the hell alone.

It doesn't take long for me to reach the center of town. I pull out my phone again, checking the time because the place I want to go has a certain time they're open. Satisfied that they're accepting customers, I stride in the direction of the second-hand store.

Two trucks are parked outside the store. As soon as I open the door, a bell rings to announce my arrival. I take in the musty scent of used clothes and pause by the door as I get a good look around.

A balding man with a comb-over and glasses too large for his face glances up at me. A frown makes his eyebrows dip under the rims. "Can I help you?" he asks.

But I keep looking. There were two trucks parked outside, meaning at least two people are in the store. It takes me only a second to find the other person.

Balanced on a ladder is a man my age – mid-thirties. His build is similar to mine, but that's where our appearances' similarities end. Where he has short-cropped dark hair, I have long, light brown hair. Stubble lines his jaw, but I keep mine clean-shaven.

He's screwing in a lightbulb, but even from here, from the set of his hard eyes to the flex of his jaw, I can tell he has demons. People like us know when we see one of our own.

As if finally aware of my presence, he glances down at me. If he's curious about me, he doesn't give it away in even a flicker of expression.

"Sir?" the man behind the counter calls again. "Is there something you're looking for?"

"Yes," is all I say. I shoulder my backpack higher, step

forward, and make my way to the men's section. I hear the man call the guy down from the ladder, giving him the name of Cole as he summons him to his side for a private chat. Probably about me. I look up from browsing shirts and find two sets of eyes on me. *Definitely about me.*

Ignoring them because I really don't give a shit, I pick up a plain black shirt that'll do. It's broad in the shoulders and, therefore, will fit mine.

In my backpack, I only have one change of clothes, and those need to be washed. Despite my leather jacket, the clothes on my back are wet from the drizzle. I have no intention of being soaked while I search for a place to stay.

There isn't much else in my backpack. A picture, a phone charger, some food, a bottle of water, and shower supplies. I don't need much. Never have.

Shirt in hand, I head to the counter under the watchful eye of both men. I set it down on the surface and flick my gaze between both men while I dig in my pocket for a few dollar bills.

The one called Cole crosses his arms over his chest and leans his spine against the wall as he studies me. The other man scowls while he rings up my shirt. "New to town?" he asks.

I give a curt nod.

"Here for business?"

I raise one eyebrow at his questions. "Pleasure." *Sort of.*

He gives me small nods while he types in the amount of the shirt into the cash register. "Don't see many guys like you around here. Derek," he introduces himself, holding out a hand for me to take. I decide to play nice and shake it. His hand is too soft against my calloused palm, and I have the sudden urge to wipe it on my black jeans. "And you are?"

"Killian," I answer gruffly.

"Well, Killian," he says, blowing out a breath and pushing

his glasses farther up his nose, "that leather jacket won't hold up to our spring. Can I interest you in a raincoat?"

The tip of his head in the direction behind me makes me slowly turn to look at what he's gesturing at. By the front door sits a rack of bright orange raincoats. Their material shines under the light of the store.

Just as slowly, I turn back around. "Orange isn't my color."

He shrugs indifferently. "Suit yourself."

I hand over my money and wait for him to give me the change. While I'm waiting, Cole grunts, "Where are you staying?"

I meet his blank expression square on. He may give nothing away on his face, but his tone says it all. It's guarded and protective. "Haven't decided yet."

"Tori Townsend just opened a B&B," Derek states while he passes me back my change. I pocket it and watch as Cole stiffens. He continues, "As far as I know, it's not currently reserved. Do you want her number?"

A bed and breakfast is a hell of a lot better than anything I had planned. I give him a curt nod, and he pulls a pad of paper from beside the register. He must have her number memorized because he jots it down quickly and passes over the paper.

I take it, study the number, and mutter my thanks as I pick up my shirt. I turn and head toward the door, listening to the two of them bicker quietly at my back. When my hand is on the door handle, I pause as Cole grunts at my back, "Killian? What's your last name?"

The corner of my lips rises. *Wouldn't you like to know?*

The bell dings when I shove the door open and step back into the drizzle. As I walk back down the sidewalk, I bring out my phone again and make the call to the B&B woman.

She answers on the third ring.

Chapter 4

Tori Townsend

I END the call and toss my phone back onto the passenger seat. Breathing deeply, I then check my side mirrors and guide my car back onto the wet road. It's not often that someone calls to rent the little house in my backyard. Whoever this Killian is, his voice was deep, gravelly, and confident, and I could tell that he was outside because of the pattering of rain and the passing of tires on wet pavement.

He hadn't said where he was from nor why he was here, and I didn't ask. When my phone rang, I'd jumped out of my skin and nearly swerved off the road. I had been so lost in thought while driving, replaying the crunch of a body hitting my hood, that the new yet abrupt sound startled me back into the present. It may not be raining like it had been last night, but the drops on my windshield were enough to bring me back to the incident.

With my mind solely occupied, I hadn't thought to ask him the important questions. All I did was agree to meet with him this morning, but first, I'll have to go to my little Wiccan store.

Most people would have taken the day off after killing someone. Tegan had tried to get me to call it off last night, but I refused. I knew a normal schedule was exactly what would heal me, and lying at home, rethinking what I'd done, would only make it worse.

I rub at my eyes and glance at my tired face in the rearview mirror. I hadn't slept a wink last night. Every time I closed my eyes, I saw hers and the dark field of lilies she sought. I look as tired as I feel.

Tegan slept over last night. She stayed up with me for as long as she could before she fell asleep in the bed beside me. Cole had left us to it, having gone home as soon as I stopped crying on Tegan's shoulders. I could tell he wanted to say something, but he never did. Perhaps it was about how taking a life wasn't easy. Or maybe how it wasn't my fault. Either way, it doesn't matter. Nothing he would have said would have made this any better. Nothing would have made me look at it differently.

I killed someone . . . and her unborn child. There are no words to soothe or smooth for that.

I pull into Mount Pleasant's downtown and frown a little when I get to my store. A rusted car has pulled up in front of the store's door, the only car in the lot. Normally, I'm the first store owner downtown every morning. I'm the first to open and the last to close, but now here is this car… and it's sitting in front of my store…

As I park in the space next to it, it hits me when I see the face of the driver. It's the kid I hired last week, and I had completely forgotten that he starts today.

Josiah Cruise turns his head and smiles shyly at me. I give him a little wave and hope like hell it isn't obvious that I forgot I had hired him in the first place.

From the interview, I remember how tall he was. A good foot above me, but that isn't saying much because I'm short. He's practically squashed in his tiny, old car like a gorilla stuffed into a monkey cage. At seventeen, he still has quite the baby face, and he hasn't lost that pudgy belly and puffy cheeks that most growing teens would have lost by now, but maybe he's a late bloomer.

His dark hair is curled like corkscrews, and he keeps it closely cropped to his head so it doesn't grow wild and in all directions. A faint shadow of a mustache is trying to make itself known above his top lip, and a few freckles are dotted on the bridge of his short nose.

From the interview, I could tell he was a nice kid. Definitely a little sheltered, which made me question why he was trying to get a job at a Wiccan shop, but it's not like I had many applicants. Kent Hilton, Pierce's grandfather, had seen to that by poisoning the area's minds into believing that I'm selling the devil's spells.

Honestly, most of the stuff I sell has to do with mind, body, and spirit. Good luck charms at worst, but Pastor Kent doesn't give a shit. He saw a target, and he went after it. I honestly don't know how much longer I'll be able to stay open if business continues to go the way it has been.

But I need Josiah because, while my shop isn't doing so great, I'm still getting plenty of business as a realtor. Yes, I have to share some of my potential customers with Kent, but my reputation is more solid than his. I've been around longer – I know the market. Because that side of my income is what's feeding me, I need reliable people to keep an eye on the shop. Tegan can't do it all, and it wouldn't be fair of me to ask.

Even from inside my car, I hear the high-pitched squeal of Josiah's door being opened. He all but squeezes his way out of the car, and with a little sigh, I slide out of my own, purse and keys in hand. I'm in a horrible mood, and I can only hope that

I don't spoil Josiah's first day. I really don't want him to think I'm that kind of boss, especially since he's a sweet kid.

"Josiah," I greet, adding a smile as we round the front of our cars to greet one another.

"Miss Townsend," he replies awkwardly. For a kid who has quite the baby face, he sure has a deep voice.

I could correct him and have him use my first name, but honestly, I like the respect of being formally addressed. I like the kid, but I don't want to be taken advantage of by youthful antics. Respect right off the bat is a good thing.

"Are you ready for your first day?" We head to the door, and I slide my key into the lock.

"Sure am."

"Good." I open the door for both of us to enter, and then I flick on the lights. My store illuminates in a soft glow that makes all the glass and glossy surfaces shine. The aroma of sage and lavender reaches my nose, and I inhale the familiar and comforting scent to chase away the lingering effects of my earlier thoughts.

Coming to work had definitely been the right move.

"I just have a few papers for you to sign before we begin," I say as I cross my store. "Give me a second to grab them."

He nods, and I disappear into the office. The office is exactly as I left it: a mess. Wrinkling my nose, I gently set my purse on the desk. It takes me a minute to find the papers, but after moving around yesterday's sandwich wrappers and chip bag, I snatch them up and head back out into the store.

Laying them on the check-out counter, I pluck up one of the pens from the cup by the register and pass it to him. He murmurs his thanks and takes the pen, and as he's filling out the paperwork, I stand there and fidget a little by pulling on my fingers. "So, uh, I never asked. What made you move to the area?"

From his application, I had seen that he moved here a month ago from the Eastern coast. Vermont or New Hampshire or somewhere up in the tip-top corner. I honestly don't remember, but I had been nosy and looked to see that the person who sold them the house was our very own resident pastor. I had been annoyed at the time because the property was just outside of the town's limits and large at that. It would have made for a good-sized commission check.

Flipping the page over, he shrugs and presses the pen back to the page. "We wanted to live in a smaller town in a more remote area. A long time ago, my great-grandparents lived in the area."

"I suppose you like being close to your family history."

He peeks at me for a split second and nods.

"So it's just you and your parents?"

With the papers filled out, he gently places the pen back into the cup and rights himself. "Just my father. My mother died when I was born."

"Ah," I say, trying not to cringe at how careless that question was. Not that I could have known, but . . . "Sorry to hear that."

He shrugs again.

"Any siblings I should plan on seeing?"

A small grin takes over his face. "I have four little brothers and sisters."

My eyebrows skyrocket into my forehead. I now have so many questions, chiefly how he could have so many younger siblings with no mother.

"Stepmother?"

He fidgets a little. "Yeah, I guess." A weird reaction, but he probably doesn't like his stepmother any better than most kids do. I didn't like my stepfather either. I could ask him; I could be nosy. Instead, I smooth out my face because it's none of my damn business.

"You must love little kids then." I clear my throat and pick up the papers. "Not many big brothers would admit to that."

"I help raise them," he says in the way of an explanation.

I pat his shoulder even though it's the height of my face. "You're a good kid, Josiah. I'm sure your parents appreciate it. Four little kids is a lot of work."

"Do you have any kids?" he asks.

I bark out a laugh. "No." *And I never want any.* Instead of saying that, I add, "I don't have the time to invest in a family."

His head bobs in small little nods, and he stuffs his hands into his jean pockets. "I dream of having a big family."

More power to you, kid. Definitely not my dream, and honestly, it shouldn't be the dream of someone who is still a kid himself, but again, I keep my mouth shut.

"So Pastor Kent sold you the property, hmm?"

"Yeah. He seems like a nice guy. Even helped us acquire chickens from another farmer. The rooster is annoying though."

I resist the urge to snort. The front door opens, and Tegan walks in. Her hair is in a messy bun, and her clothes are wrinkled, but she has a bag of donuts in her hand, so I can't fault her for her appearance. "Ah," I breathe, glad for a change of subject. "Josiah, this is Tegan. She's going to be training you until you get the hang of things."

Josiah turns around and gives a small, saluting wave.

"Hi," Tegan says quickly to him. She hands me the bag of donuts and straightens out her shirt. The action does nothing for the wrinkles. I left my house before she did, so I imagine that she ran home and dressed as quickly as she could, and this is just the result. "I'm always late, aren't I?"

I scratch the back of my neck, deciding not to answer that. Instead, I take the donuts to the office and call over my shoulder, "Why don't you have a look around, Josiah? We'll be right back."

Close on my heels, Tegan follows me into the office and shuts the door behind us. She crowds me as I sit down at my desk and move my finger across the mouse pad to wake up my laptop. As soon as it lights up, it displays the two cameras' feeds.

Tegan squints over my shoulder. "When did you get cameras?"

"The other day," I say with a sigh.

"Why?"

I glance at her. "With Kent next door, I thought it was wise."

Her lips twist. "Makes sense. That's kind of a smart idea."

"I have a few of those sometimes. I even got a camera for my house."

She chuckles under her breath. "And you think I'm the paranoid one."

Loosely, I cross my arms over my chest. "Well, if you had someone hell-bent on destroying everything you've worked so hard for, you would have cameras too."

"True." Her mouth puckers in thought. "He'll get bored of you eventually."

"Pierce said the same thing to me once. God, I hope so."

She studies me for a moment before grabbing a donut out of the bag and taking a generous bite. "How is the sheriff anyway?"

"He seemed fine last night."

"Is he still trying to get back in your pants?"

I roll my eyes. "We both were a little too busy last night to even think about that. Besides, the sex with Pierce was okay, but not memorable enough for a second round. Although . . . I do miss the handcuffs."

"Hussy."

"Look, I picked up a cucumber the other day, and my nipples got hard."

She shakes her head. "I think you're too kinky to be my best friend."

I lift an eyebrow. "Says the woman who likes to be choked while she's railed."

"You have a drawer full of toys. You don't need a vegetable." Around a mouthful, she smiles, swallows, and then her expression turns thoughtful. "How are you doing anyway?"

My shrug is small. I look down at the keyboard of my laptop, and my voice is small as I say, "I'm alright."

"No, you're not."

I wet my bottom lip and stretch out my tense neck. "I will be."

She is quiet for a few moments before she softly adds, "I'm here if you need me. You know that, right?"

I raise my gaze to give her a small smile that definitely doesn't reach my eyes. "I know."

She returns the expression before picking up the bag of donuts and passing it to me. "Nothing a little frosting can't fix."

Even though I don't feel it, I chuckle and take the offered bag. "I should really stop eating these."

"Why?"

I scowl up at her and then wave a hand down my torso.

She looks heavenward and snorts. "You are *not* fat. There's just a little more of you to love."

My chuff is loud and completely unladylike. "I'll try to remember that."

"As you should."

I lift the donut to my lips, take a bite, and chew thoughtfully. "Are you going to be okay training him alone?"

She scowls. "Why? Do you have somewhere you have to be?"

I nod. "Some guy wants to rent the B&B. I have to meet up with him here in a bit."

She waves me off. "No problem. He seems like an easy-going kid anyway."

"Awesome," I say tiredly. I take another generous bite,

stand up, and give her a kiss on the cheek full of crumbs, all of which she wipes away dramatically. Grabbing my purse off my desk, I give her a little wave as I head out. “Thanks,” I add over my shoulder.

“Mhmm,” I hear her hum.

Chapter 5

Killian Savage

I STAND in front of Tori Townsend's home, grasping both backpack straps on my shoulders and giving them a good squeeze. It looks a lot like my old house before I sold it and left without a backward glance. *Before,* when everything was normal. As normal as my life outwardly appeared anyway.

Her house is one story. The dark siding is a stark contrast to the white trim, and the flowers chosen for the flowerbeds are something someone I once knew would have planted. It doesn't have a porch, only steps that lead to the front door.

The grass is neatly trimmed, and as far as I can tell, there isn't a weed in sight, which tells me she either has it cared for or she has a green thumb. My bet is the former. I looked her up on my walk over here. She's a businesswoman, and I doubt she has time to mow and weed.

The front yard is a decent size. The house sits closer to the crumbling sidewalk to give room for the space in the back. A path leads from the gravel driveway to the front door, and a little birdbath sits directly under a large bay window that has the curtains open.

I never had a birdbath at my house, but it's a nice touch, especially if you have the time to watch the creatures come and go.

On either side of the window, almost growing across the space, are two neatly trimmed fur trees.

I glance around and realize that this is the nicest house on the block. It doesn't scream expense, but it sure shows that at least the outside was renovated, whether that be by her or the previous owner.

Curious about the inside and the woman who lives here, I cross the lawn, step into the rock garden, and move a fur's branches out of the way. I cup my hand around my eyes and get a good look inside.

Through the window, I see the living room. It holds newer furniture, and the walls look like they've been painted recently, but past the living room is the kitchen. Unlike the outside of the house, the kitchen was untouched; plain and light yellow cabinets and dark green counters. The stove looks new but inexpensive, and a black tea kettle is sitting on top of it.

The kettle reminds me of the same person I try hard not to think about, and I back away from the window like my mind backs away from the memory.

I step out of the rocks and head to the driveway in search of this B&B. At the end of the driveway is a small house. It's not large enough to have bedrooms. If I had to guess, everything is in one room.

The siding matches the house, but it has no rock garden and no vegetation. Just like the house, the curtains are open, so I stride to it and study the inside. I breathe out through my nose when I see that my suspicions are correct. The bed, the kitchen, and the small living space are all in one room. The only door in the place is that which leads to the bathroom.

It's better than most places I've slept since I left New York.

The room reveals that it was decorated with a woman's touch, too – floral printed pictures and mountain paintings. The bed has a cheap black comforter, but there are many pillows in a variety of sizes to choose from.

I hear a car driving down the damp street, so I turn and rest my back against the B&B's outer wall. Seconds later, a light blue Chevelle pulls onto the driveway. The tires crunch against the gravel as it slowly pulls up. I frown because that is definitely not a car I thought the woman on the phone would drive.

The roar of the engine cuts off as she parks beside the house. A glare on the windshield prevents me from seeing what she looks like until she opens the door and lifts herself out of it.

I blink as I'm again reminded of that very person, and for a moment, all words get stuck in my throat. The woman walking in my direction has short blonde hair and slight facial features that accentuate her round blue eyes. She's not tall, and the dress she's wearing would probably drag on the ground if she wasn't holding it up. Her hips sway confidently, thick hips that I have trouble taking my eyes away from.

"Are you Killian?" she asks. Her tone is tired, and it's enough for me to return my gaze to hers.

I clear my throat from the clog that's formed there and push off the wall. "Yeah," is my only answer.

She stops in front of me, releases her dress, and props her hands on her hips. "I'm Tori. Welcome to Fairview."

"Thanks," I mumble. A little louder, I add, "Interesting choice of a car. Is it your husband's?"

She bristles, bunching her shoulders close to her ears. I must have hit a nerve. "Not married and not my car. I got into an accident last night," she pauses to swallow thickly. "Borrowed this hunk of junk from a friend."

I remain still because I remember reading about that accident. It never said who it involved, but someone died. It has to be the same accident because, in this small town, I doubt there are many, and on the same day at that.

It's on the tip of my tongue, the desire to ask her about it, but I somehow manage to refrain.

She stands there for a moment, studying me like everyone else does. But unlike most people, instead of fear, I see curiosity. She studies the tattoos on my hands and then the backpack on my shoulders. "Is that all you brought?"

"I have everything I need."

"In one backpack?"

I give one curt nod.

Her eyebrows raise into her forehead, and she lets out a breath. "Okay then. There can't be many clothes in there, so if you need a washing machine, just let me know. The only one is in the main house."

I remain silent and flex my jaw a little. I hadn't planned on asking her for anything. It's against my nature to ask for help.

She cocks her head to the side. "Why are you here anyway? You don't seem the type to hike or fish."

"I'm not."

"Then why are you in Fairview?"

My shrug is my immediate answer.

She leans forward on the balls of her feet. "I need a little more information, Killian. You'll be living behind me."

"I'm just passing through."

"Okay," she says, drawing out the word. "There's no car here. Did you walk?"

"Some."

"From?"

I sigh and pinch the bridge of my nose. "New York."

She curses in a hissing sort of way. "Why the hell Fairview?"

I drop my hand back to my side. "Like I said, I'm just passing through. Do you ask these questions to everyone who rents from you?"

She holds up a finger. "First of all, my bed and breakfast isn't exactly a busy place. People prefer to stay in the cabins. And secondly, I'm a single woman, and you don't look like you're very friendly. It wouldn't be smart to not ask questions."

My lips twitch to the side because I can see her point. She's a beautiful woman, and the more I stand in front of her, the more interesting she becomes. Her facial expressions are out in the open, unhidden and raw, and the power and confidence she exudes are unmatched by most women. I find that it challenges my own, and I don't know whether I like that or not, but it's definitely intriguing.

Her arms cross over her chest, and she rolls her head to stretch her neck out. "I'll need your ID."

"Why?" I demand.

"Because you'll be renting from me." She rolls her eyes as if the answer should be obvious. "If you skip out on payment, I can have you hunted down. No ID, no place to stay."

I clench my jaw again, release my backpack from my shoulders, and dig around in the front pocket. Once I have my wallet grasped in my palm, I drop the backpack to the ground, open the flap, and dig out my ID. I pass it to her without a word.

She reads the name. "Killian Savage. That doesn't sound too friendly either."

"Maybe I'm not a friendly guy."

"If you tell me about yourself, I can be the judge of that." A ghost of a smile plays on her lips, but it doesn't reach her eyes.

"I'm just passing through," I say again, hoping she gets the hint. While I may have the desire to learn more about her, she doesn't need to know about me. No one needs to know about me, what I've done, and the kind of man that I am. It's nothing to be proud of.

"Right," she whispers, narrowing her eyes. "And how long do you plan to stay?"

"A week, maybe two."

"That's a long time for someone who is just passing through."

I shrug again. It's been a long journey, and I need the sleep before I wear out my body, before I continue my search for the man who doesn't seem to exist. But she doesn't need to know all that. All she needs to know is that I'm a drifter, a wanderer, and we'll leave it at that.

"Okay," she grumbles a little when I say nothing in return. She passes me a single key from the depths of her palm and adds, "I'll scan your ID and give it back to you. I swear to god, Killian, if you give me any trouble…"

"I'm just passing through," I murmur again.

She shakes her head. "Well, I hope you find Fairview to your liking. If you need anything, just call or knock on my door."

"Thanks," I all but whisper.

As she backs away toward her house, I turn to the door and slide the key into the hole. Pausing, I glance over my shoulder and watch her disappear into the main house. Something tells me that not giving her any information about me will only stir the need to find out more. All I can hope is that I'm dead wrong about that.

Chapter 6

Tori Townsend

AS FAR AS I KNOW, Killian has been gone all day. After our interaction this morning, he had dropped his backpack inside the B&B and took off on foot toward downtown. Am I ashamed that I watched his backside until he disappeared around the corner? Absolutely not.

It's truly a fine ass. Round, firm. It deserves my attention.

I peek discreetly through the blinds while he strides up my driveway. Even from this side of the wall, I can hear his feet crunch on the gravel. His stride is confident, and since the drizzle has stopped for the time being, he has his jacket tucked into the crook of his elbow. Even in the darkness, I can see his arms covered in tattoos.

It does nothing to sway my initial thought that he might be trouble.

And, damn it, I find it completely hot. I've always been a sucker for the walking red flags.

I pull away from the window as he passes by it and look at my laptop that's sitting open on my dining room table. The camera feed is up, and it might be a little embarrassing that I've been waiting for him to return. Where the hell did he go? What did he do all day? And why the hell doesn't he have a car?

I mean, who the hell walks everywhere?

Leaning a little toward the screen, I watch as he unlocks the B&B's door, but for a split second, he swivels his gaze toward the camera. He stares at it for a moment, almost as though he knows I'm staring at him and he's daring me with it.

The rugged lines of his face cast shadows across his neck and features. Around here, you don't find men like him, and you sure as hell don't find men who have hair long enough for a man-bun. With the grooves of his large, muscular arms covered in ink, his confident stride, and the power he exudes, it'd be a miracle if people didn't give him a wide berth.

It should make me want to steer clear of him, but I'm already thinking of ways I can approach him again.

Ever since my ex, I've never been this drawn to a man. My ex was nothing like Killian, of course. He was the exact opposite in physique and demeanor, but he was trouble. A bad boy. I told myself I'd never get involved with someone like that because, in the end, all bad boys do is break your heart just like my ex did to me when he used me to sell my identity for extra pocket cash to pay for his weed.

My ex may have gone to jail for a few years, but if you ask me, he deserved far more than that for making me believe he loved me.

I haven't felt something for a guy since. I don't need a therapist to realize that I have issues when it comes to men, issues when it comes to things of deep commitment. Like marriage for example. *No way*. My ex screwed that over for me, ruined that dream my little girl self once had of a happily-ever-after and riding off into the sunset with a man I'd be deeply in love with.

Killian looks back to the door and opens it. I hold my breath until he's inside, and I plop down in the dining room chair when he closes it behind him.

Even through a camera, he holds me captive.

I'm in serious trouble.

My gaze drifts to his ID. I haven't given it back to him yet. Of course, I've researched him, but all I've found was an address he once had in New York, New York. It's the address on his ID, and there are no previous addresses before that. In my assessment, he had been a man of commitment, but what had changed? What made him sell his home and drift this far west?

I'll never get those answers, not unless I seek further help. I bite my bottom lip as I look to my right where my phone rests beside my laptop. It takes me a few seconds, but I pick it up, swipe in my password, and bring up Pierce's number. I press the dial button before I can think better of it.

He picks up on the third ring. "Tori? Is everything okay?"

I cringe a little. I don't call him. Ever. The only reason I have his number is because I didn't want to be a bitch when he gave it to me the night we slept together. "Yeah, sorry. Um-"

"How are you? Are you doing okay?"

I know he means about the woman I killed, but honestly, I haven't thought much about it since this morning, thanks to the puzzle that is Killian. He's been a good distraction.

"I'm okay." Even to my own ears, my tone is unconvincing.

"Are you sure? I can come over, and we can talk?"

I wave a hand in the air as if he can see me as my heart drops to my toes because he just might despite my protests. "That's not necessary, and I swear it's not why I called. I'm doing okay, I promise."

There's a long pause, and I'm sure the rejections stung a little. I cringe while I wait for him to say something, and when he finally does, I let out a slow breath. "Then what's up?" I can hear the disappointment in his voice, but I brush it aside because I don't have room in me to endure another emotion at the moment.

"I have someone who is renting my B&B," I begin.

"That's good," he answers. I hear the phone rustle on his end. "Some business is always good."

"Yeah," I answer as I peek at the closed blinds. I blurt, "I want you to look into him."

"What?"

"Research him." I regret the words as soon as I say them because, if roles were reversed, I'd want my peace instead of someone sifting through my life. But for some odd reason, I continue because it's also my personal safety and my business's reputation in question. If he's going to be a problem, I need to know. "Pick apart his past. Background checks and all that."

He chuckles as if he thinks I'm not being serious. When I don't laugh with him, he murmurs, "Wait. Really?"

"Yes," I answer with clarity.

"Why?"

I twist my lips to the side, wondering how much I should tell him because, really, all I have are opinions and suspicion, and a whole lot of attraction. "Because he wasn't very forthcoming about why he was here."

"That's not enough reason, Tori."

I frown. "Look, I just want to make sure that he doesn't cause trouble. I want to know who the man is that's sleeping in my backyard."

"Alright, alright." The phone makes a weird sound when he blows out a breath. "I can see what I can find. What's his name?"

"Killian Savage. He's from New York, New York."

"Okay. I'll look into it in my free time, but Tori?"

"Hmm?"

"I wouldn't think much of it. Anyone who causes trouble

isn't going to come to Fairview. That would be mighty random."

"Need I remind you of the old sheriff who now sits in jail?" The previous sheriff is rotting behind bars for murder and attempted murder. He'll die of old age in there for his crimes, and that's only if the inmates don't shank him first.

He sighs. "Besides him."

"Right."

"Why don't you get some sleep? I'm sure you need it after last night."

I scowl but say, "Yeah, you're probably right," because I don't want the topic of the woman brought up again. Not when I have the distraction that is the secretive hot man behind my house. Not when it's serving me so well.

"I am right. Goodnight, Tori."

"Night," I respond, and then I hang up.

As soon as I move to set my phone back down on the table, my phone pings with an incoming text. I sigh as I read Tegan's message. She's promising to bring donuts to work tomorrow, and while this once made me grateful, I really need to think about eating more healthily again. But I know she's just trying to take care of me. I know that, by the way she's doing it, she thinks she's looking after me without trying to be obvious about it.

So instead of asking her not to, I thank her and tell her I'll see her in the morning. She'll probably be late again like she always is, but I honestly expect it now. It doesn't bother me. She's my best friend, and I know she means well.

Chapter 7

Killian Savage

I LEAN against the wall of one of the many buildings downtown that have long since closed their business. This particular building has a 'for sale' sign on it, bright red and right in my face. The sun glares off of it. However, I ignore it in favor of a different view.

My gaze doesn't leave Tori. I hadn't followed her. It was a coincidence that she showed up downtown in her borrowed and loud Chevelle at the same time that I arrived here. I watch as she parks the car and gathers her purse from the passenger side.

It's been two days since I arrived in Fairview. I've come and gone from the B&B as I pleased, but sometimes, at night, I can tell she's watching me. Someone like me grows a sixth sense to things like that, knowing when they're being watched. Truth be told, the blinds overlooking the driveway sometimes move as I stride up the gravel.

She's curious about me. I'd be lying if I said I wasn't curious about her too, more so as to why she's not afraid of me. The way she gave me back my ID was interesting though. Instead of waiting to pass it to me in person, she stuck it in the crack of the B&B's front door.

I shift a little, placing my balance on one foot before moving to the other. She could have easily gone inside and searched my belongings to appease her curiosity. It's not like she would have found much besides stuff that would bring about more questions – the picture, for example. The fact that she didn't, tells me I might be a little wrong about her. She's untrusting, that much is blatantly obvious, but not so much so that she'd invade someone's immediate privacy. Especially someone like me, who refused to give her any of the answers she sought.

She's parked in front of the donut shop, and I can smell the fried dough from here. I tried one yesterday when the place wasn't as packed as it is now. I've never been one for crowds, so when I saw that it was empty, I went in to appease my stomach from the aroma that slithers through the entire downtown atmosphere.

With her purse slid over her shoulder, she gets out of the car. The door squeals as it opens, and her floral dress pools around her ankles when her flip-flops are on firm ground.

My gaze doesn't move from her when a beat-up truck pulls up and parks beside her car. Only when she turns a smile in their direction do I look and see who the newcomers are.

A blonde woman hops out of the passenger side before the driver shuts off the truck. She has blonde hair, just like Tori's, and is a little thicker around the waist than Tori as well. But even I know what I see: the rosy cheeks and that glow the skin gives off. The slight swell above the pubic bone. The exhausted under eyes from restless nights of worrying.

I remember the first signs of pregnancy well.

I cross my arms over my chest as the driver climbs out of his seat and shuts the door behind him. For a moment, our eyes meet. Even from where I stand, I can see Cole's jaw flex.

I knew he didn't like me the moment I met him in the thrift store, but I hadn't expected him to remember me after the moment I left.

The blonde woman says something to him, causing him to look at her for a split second and nod. His eyes return to mine, however, and I don't back down from his challenging stare. There's an air about the way he tenses his features that's telling of the man beneath. Just like at the thrift store, I recognize it because darkness knows darkness.

Cole says something to the women, and they link arms and head inside the donut shop. Once they're inside, Cole strides my way.

I don't move as he crosses the street with purposeful steps, gaze locked on mine. I won't give him the satisfaction of thinking he has rattled me by his approach because, honestly, I've met worse. Not a whole lot scares me these days.

He stops just before me and matches my stance with his arms crossing over his chest. "Cole," I greet gruffly.

He makes a grunting sound at the back of his throat. "What are you doing here, Killian?"

I raise an eyebrow because where I'm at and why I'm there is none of his damn business. "Going for a stroll."

His eyes narrow a little. "Looked to me like you were watching Tori."

My shrug is nonchalant. "And what if I was?"

Cole's jaw flexes, and it ripples his cheeks. "I don't know why you're in town, but I recommend that you don't stay long."

"And why is that?"

"Things just started turning around here," he divulges in a tense sort of way. "And if you have an interest in Tori, leave it be."

"Why is Tori any of your concern?" I ask, pushing off the wall and pocketing my hands into my jeans.

"She's my wife's friend. That makes her my concern."

"Touching," I mumble, gaze swiveling to the shop's windows. I vaguely see Tori inside, taking a seat at a table with Cole's wife. She's chatting with her, and a faint smile ghosts her lips. It's then that I realize that I've never seen a true smile from her. It's almost like it can never reach her eyes, as though something troubles her to keep her from doing so. From experience, I recognize that too.

"The last guy she dated stole her identity," he nearly growls at my brush-off. "You look like you'd do worse."

His words echo my thoughts. I turn my attention back to him, eyebrows raised. "It's not any of your damn business, but I'm not interested in a relationship."

"Good," he grunts. "Then stay away from her."

I cock my head to the side. "Are you trying to protect Tori from me? Or your wife from me?"

There's that jaw flex again, but he says nothing. Probably because it's both.

"How far along is she?" I ask threateningly. I don't like that he approached me, and I definitely don't like that he thinks he can order me around. I'd never hurt a pregnant woman, but he doesn't have to know that.

"Leave her out of this."

I raise both hands. "Then leave me out of it."

"How could you possibly know that she's pregnant? She hasn't told anyone."

Sighing, I tip my head toward the shop's window where both women still sit. "Just because I'm alone *now* doesn't mean I was alone *before.*"

And with that, I step away from Cole and begin to walk away. I have no interest in an extended argument for something that'll never happen between Tori and myself. I may be attracted to her, but I didn't come here to look for a piece of ass. It would just complicate things when I drifted off and disappeared without a backward glance.

I pause in my stride as Cole says to my back, "Killian?" I turn my head. "Don't stay here for long. I meant what I said."

There was no threat or warning in his tone. I don't know if what I said touched something inside him that broke through that outer protective shell he wears, but that part had faded from his tone. So, instead of challenging him, I give a curt nod because, if roles were reversed, I wouldn't want someone like me near my wife either.

I don't take it for granted because, if Cole knew exactly who I am and what I've done, he would have escorted me out by now. What I'd done cost me everything I had. He'd fear for what he has in return just by my mere presence in this small, sleepy town. And if he knew why I'm drifting, if he knew what I had planned once I found the man who wronged me, who stole my life from me, he wouldn't be so sympathetic.

Something tells me he'd go beyond the law to make sure I never came back here. Maybe even make sure I disappeared for good.

That should scare me, but it doesn't.

He says nothing more, so I step forward, glancing only once at the donut shop's window and waiting for my demons to rise within at the mere thought of my past and the woman who reminds me of it.

Chapter 8

Tori Townsend

"THE LILIES CAME IN BEAUTIFULLY," I say to Tegan as I take a sip of coffee.

The donut shop is full of people this morning, and although I usually like to be surrounded by people because I'm an extrovert, I just have no interest this morning.

All night last night, I dreamed of eyes staring at me under the shine of headlights as well as the sounds of the accident. That wasn't the only thing I dreamed about though. I received small reprieves with the man in my backyard. The leather jacket. The faint smell of him that the wind brought to me. The intense expressions he wears. Even my subconscious is curious about him. Maybe a little more than curious.

I take a quick glance around at the patrons to force my mind to drift in a different direction than Killian. Cole already left to go do some work on one of Derek's rentals, leaving me and Tegan alone to talk. I can tell by the way she's fidgeting in her seat that she wants to say something, but so far, she hasn't said anything important in her attempt at small talk.

I'll be driving her to my store today, and Cole will be picking her up after her shift. I love my time with my best friend, but I can't stand the stolen, concerned glances. They hurt worse than the dreams. They're just a reminder of what I've done when all I want is to pretend that things are normal. More than anything, I want to act like it didn't happen because, maybe if I do, I won't feel like this. This empty feeling, this hollowed-out self.

She sets down her glass of juice. "I didn't expect them to bloom so well. Must be all the rain."

I give her a small smile that I know doesn't reach my eyes because the only way that I know that they're beautiful is thanks to the car crash. I may have only seen them in the dark, but they were stunning.

I've been thinking about going there to think and maybe find some sort of closure. I just haven't had the guts to yet. At least, not alone.

She must know I need a change of subject because she asks, "Is Josiah working today?"

"I offered for him to, but I left it up to him. He never said if he was going to or not."

"He seems like a nice kid."

I nod. "I think I got lucky there."

She takes a bite of her donut. After she swallows, she adds, "Most kids his age aren't as hardworking, but I think he has a thing for you. Aim to impress and all that." She chuckles and dusts sprinkles off her sleeve.

"What?" I blink, shocked. "What makes you say that?"

She shrugs, but a smile grows on her face. "He asks a lot of questions about you. Innocent questions, but it's cute."

"Great," I mumble, flare my nostrils, and look away.

Her laugh is musical. "It's a little crush and it's adorable. Just take it as a compliment."

I sigh and look back at my friend. "That's not what I need right now."

Her smile fades at the seriousness of my tone, and she reaches for my hand. When she takes it into hers, she murmurs, "Do you want to talk yet?"

"There's nothing to talk about." How do I tell her that my debt will never be paid? How do I tell her that no amount of listening will ever change the fact that I killed someone? It's something I'll always have to live with and a situation that I'll have to find a way to make peace with, but only on my own.

She closes her eyes in frustration, but she still gives my hand a squeeze. When she opens them, she takes back her hand. "Okay. But I'm here."

"I know," I whisper.

I was so lost in the direction of our conversation that I didn't see the shop's door open and the person who strode in. Not until he's by our side and his cologne takes up our space.

Glancing up in surprise, I greet Pierce. "Hey," I say clearly. He's clean-shaven, and his uniform is wrinkle-free. As always, he's well put together.

"Sheriff," Tegan says, forcing the corner of her lips to tilt up. Though he's done nothing to her, it's obvious that she isn't a fan of him. I don't blame her. If I was shot by a sheriff, I wouldn't trust another one again either. But Pierce is a good guy, and as far as I can tell, he doesn't wish harm on anyone. He's not like the last sheriff, a slimy bastard who had the wool pulled over all our eyes until he put a bullet into Tegan's back.

"Ladies," he greets back. Dutifully, he ignores Tegan's expression. "Enjoying breakfast?"

Both of us nod. "What are you doing here?" I know that he doesn't drink coffee, and he's more of a health nut. I've never seen a donut in his hand.

He swivels his hips to face me better. "I came to talk to you, actually. I saw the car out front and decided a face-to-face conversation was better than a phone call."

I scowl a little. "About what?"

Sneaking a glance at Tegan, he rocks back on his heels. "Think we can talk in private?"

I turn my scowl to Tegan, who only narrows her eyes at him. "Whatever you're going to say," I begin, looking back at him, "You can say in front of her because there's a one-hundred-percent chance that I'm going to tell her anyway."

His lips thin out. I know he's not happy about that, but honestly, I can't deal with another 'go out with me' conversation. Tegan would be a good buffer when I turn him down again. "It's about the woman."

"From the accident?" Tegan asks when I sit there too long, feeling punched in the gut while I blink rapidly at Pierce.

He nods but keeps his studying gaze on me. "Are you sure you don't want this to be private?"

I bite my bottom lip but shake my head as I push a hand through my hair. "No, no. Like I said, I'll end up telling her anyway."

"Okay, if you're sure," he says, drawing out the sentence. He sucks in a breath and crosses his arms over his chest.

"I am."

Tegan leans a little closer to him and lowers her voice. "What did you find out?"

"There was no identification on her," he starts.

"Fingerprints?" I ask. With any hope, she was in the system.

My hopes are dashed when he gives a small shake of his head. "Her teeth were removed, and her fingerprints were burned."

Tegan curses under her breath.

"We did find one thing though: the branding. Did you see the lily tattooed on her wrist?"

"How is that going to help?" I ask because it was just a flower. A weird coincidence that she died in front of a field of lilies, but still, just a flower.

His eyebrows pull down. "I don't know, but it's one more thing we do know about her than we knew before."

It's a little concerning that someone went so far as to remove any way to identify her, and it does nothing to squash this guilt inside me. I don't know what I was hoping for, but if we can't find her family, there's nothing I can do to apologize.

"And the baby?" I ask softly.

He swallows thickly, and I can tell he doesn't want to say what he's going to mutter next. "She was eight months pregnant. A boy."

I look down at the steam coming out of the hole in the lid on my coffee. A lump forms in my throat, and the threat of tears pricks my eyes.

Pierce places a gentle hand on my shoulder. "It wasn't your fault, Tori," he whispers sympathetically. "She was running from whoever was in that van. You just happened to be there, and it just happened to be you who…"

"Killed her," I finish for him, my tone as dead as I feel.

He crouches so that he's more at eye level with me. "We found bruises around her wrists, on her knees, and along the bones of her ankles. She was being held captive." Tegan gasps, but he continues, "With how far along she was, she wouldn't have been able to run far from that man. I know it doesn't help any, but chances are you set her free."

I swipe away a tear angrily. What he said does nothing to squash the guilt. "What's being done to look for the man?" His bright orange coat flashes in my mind, and it's enough to make me look into Pierce's eyes.

He twists his lips to the side for a moment. "We're looking for black vans in the area, but so far, we haven't come up with anything. They may have just been passing through."

I give him small nods even though all I want to do is yell at him. It's not his fault that he knows nothing, and I know that, but I'm frustrated. Someone needs to be brought to justice.

"What's being done with her body since you can't find any family?"

He balances his elbows on his knees and pops his knuckles. "She'll be cremated and then buried in the cemetery."

Swiping away more tears, I frown and blurt, "Give her ashes to me."

"What?" Tegan and Pierce say together.

"I'm not giving up on her." My voice is clear and confident. "And until the family is found, I'll hang on to the ashes so they can bury her where she lived."

He stares at me for a moment, eyes taking in my face, but he says, "Okay. If you're sure."

"I'm sure." I can tell Tegan wants to protest, so I switch the subject before she can. "Did you find anything out about Killian?"

He rises back up and crosses his arms back over his chest. "I've been busy with the woman, but I plan to look into him today."

"You're having your B&B guy looked into?" Tegan asks, exasperated.

"Maybe." I cringe a little, but my guilt transfers from the accident to the invasion of privacy. It's a welcome transition because one hurts more than the other.

"If you want to come by the station, I'll bring food, and we can look into him together," Pierce asks innocently. I'm not a fool though. I know what a date sounds like.

Tegan's eyes widen, but I shake my head at Pierce. "I have too much going on, and I trust that you'll be able to find out about him without my help."

His expression puckers for a moment, as if he just sucked on a lemon wedge. "If you're sure."

I clear my throat a little, ridding the rest of the tears so that he takes me seriously when I proclaim, "I am."

Rubbing his neck, he sighs. "Well, I'll let you know what I find then."

"Thanks," I say quickly, effectively dismissing him. He gets the hint, tips his head at us in farewell, and strides out of the shop.

When he's gone, Tegan whispers, "Ouch," with a grin.

I take a sip from my coffee. "I don't know how much clearer I can be."

She lifts her donut to her lips. "So you're really looking into him?"

"I shouldn't, and yet, I am."

Her cheeks bulge from the bite until she chews and swallows it down. "Cole doesn't like him either."

"How does Cole know who he is?" I ask, cocking my head to the side.

"He met him with Derek. He said the interaction was brief, but it was enough for Cole to decide he didn't like what he saw."

"Interesting," I mumble. I run my finger along the rim of my cup's lid.

I glance up when she adds, "But if you ask me, I think you should give him a chance."

I lift my chin and look down from my cheekbones at her. "And why is that?"

"Well, for one, I've never seen you this interested in a guy, albeit he might be some bad guy. And two, I know from personal experience not to judge a book by its cover."

My eyebrows flick up into my forehead for a split second, and I lower my head back down. "True. Well shit, now I feel horrible."

"For?" she asks, licking some frosting from her fingertip.

"For having Pierce look into him."

Waving a hand in the air, she chuckles. "Honestly, I just think you're fascinated by him."

I tuck my lips between my teeth and refuse to answer that. Instead, I lean to grab my purse from the floor and dig around inside for my phone. When I grasp it, I yank it out and swipe through my password.

"What are you doing?" she asks, leaning into the table to try to peer over it.

"Telling Pierce that I've changed my mind."

"I doubt that's going to stop him from looking into him."

I glance up at her. "Maybe." I curse under my breath. "I knew it was a mistake to ask for his help in the first place, but now I feel like a horrible person for invading Killian's privacy. He's done nothing to deserve it."

She wipes a growing smile from her face with a napkin.

"What?" I demand when she doesn't say anything.

"Nothing," she quickly says.

I set my phone on the table. "Spit it out, Tegan."

"Well..." She shifts a little in her seat. "Normally. you don't care about this kind of thing. Why is Killian any different?"

I scratch at my cheek as I think it over. I mean, I know the answer to that – I'm curious about Killian. However, I'm not going to tell her that because she'll read too much into it. More into it than I'm even ready to admit to myself because calling myself a whore is just a little too much for me right now.

She chuckles under her breath, and I open my mouth to deny whatever she's thinking, but she shoves the last of the donut into her mouth and stands up. Around a mouthful of food, she says, "Come on. We're going to be late."

Chapter 9

Killian Savage

SUNSET HAS CAST the clouds into a pale-pink hue across the majority of the sky, but on the horizon, dark rain clouds threaten. The rain just won't quit here, but at least today, this part of Utah has had a small break from it.

With my hands stuffed in my jacket pockets, I stroll up the middle of the street, not bothering with the sidewalk. Dogs and their owners walk the sidewalk, and I've learned the hard way that dogs don't find me . . . approachable.

Dogs are said to be a good judge of character, so they're probably right. It doesn't matter. I had never been interested in owning a pet because I was always working. I could have brought the pet with me to my job, but for what I did . . . Not even a cat needs to witness that.

Tori's house comes into view, and as I get closer, I hear cursing. My brows pinch together until I'm on her driveway. The hood to the Chevelle is popped open, and she's leaning over the engine. I stand at the end for a moment, observing her ass as soft curses filter in my direction.

It's the perfect shape, like a peach, and just like a peach, it begs to be bitten into.

I scrub at the stubble along my jaw and start my way toward her. I can tell she has no idea what she's doing. Hell, I can tell she doesn't know what she's even looking for by the way she uses her phone's flashlight, searching.

She doesn't hear my shoes crunching on the gravel, and when I come to a stop behind her, she doesn't even notice my presence.

"This is just stupid," she grumbles. "Give me a fucking lemon for a car."

I clear my throat, and she nearly jumps out of her skin. She spins around so fast that she teeters for a second. I snatch my hand out and grip her upper arm to keep her from falling over. Her skin is soft under my firm touch, and my eyes zero in on the contact. I hadn't meant to touch her. It was pure instinct, but now that I have . . .

I don't want to let go.

"You scared the shit out of me," she whispers. There's no anger in it, and the soft tone is enough to pull my attention back to her. The expression on her face is inquisitive. Her lips are slightly parted, but when she slowly slides her gaze to the contact, I gently let her go.

She probably didn't appreciate the lingering touch. As I bring my hand back to my side, she raises her eyes back to mine, and I watch as her throat constricts with a heavy swallow.

Or maybe she did appreciate it.

Interesting indeed. Not only is she curious about me, but she's attracted to me. Not many women are, but she doesn't seem like most women, and I can't be the only thing she's endlessly curious about. A restless soul, just like someone I once knew. A touch of obsession that was never satisfied until she had answers. And right now, she's zeroed in on me.

I don't know if I should be defensive about it or let her have her fun.

"Sorry," I murmur.

She pushes her hair up behind her ear and straightens her oversized graphic t-shirt over the hem of her sweatpants. I've never seen her dressed down, but I like the look. It makes her seem less boss-like and more human. Not that I don't like her bossy personality, but seeing her raw and vulnerable like this . . . It does something to me. So much so that I take one small step back, away from where my thoughts are taking me and the very fine object that's bringing them about.

"It's fine," she breathes out.

I look at the engine so that I'm not sweeping her body with my gaze. "Car trouble?"

"Yes," she hisses. "Derek gave me a shit car." Her shoulders sag, and a defeated and tired look relaxes her face. "I should be grateful that he gave me one at all, but nothing seems to be going right for me. Everyone is trying to help, and that should make me happy, but it doesn't, and now all these terrible things are happening to me, and my life is a shit show that you should just ignore because . . . "

I glance at her, and for a moment, our eyes connect. She searches the depths of mine as I do hers. If this were my life before, I'd pull her into my arms to stop the tears that are threatening the corners of her eyes. But this isn't my 'before.' That still doesn't stop me from appreciating her presence. However, her being in my space… It makes my spine tingle with goosebumps even if she is upset.

"I'm sorry," she whispers, breaking the eye contact. Her head bends forward a little. "I just vomited all my problems onto you."

"Sounds like a lot of problems."

She blows out a breath, and a traitorous tear tumbles down her cheek. She wipes it away angrily. "You have no idea."

The urge to reach out and rub the rest of the wetness away is strong, but instead, I clench my jaw and turn to the car. No matter how much she reminds me of *her*, I cannot give in because I'm not finished with what I started out to do when I left New York.

And yet, I still ask, "Want to talk about it?" I don't know why I said it. It just came out, like an automatic response.

I see her shake her head. "You shouldn't be burdened with my problems."

I nod a little because I can understand that. I don't tell people about my problems either. "So what's wrong with the car?"

She faces the hood with me. "It's weird when it starts."

"How so?"

Using her hands to gesture wildly, she explains the troubles the car has. It takes half her speech to already know what's wrong, but I let her prattle on because I know she needs it. When she's finished, I close the hood, and she turns a frown in my direction. "What are you doing?"

"You need new spark plugs."

She loosely crosses her arms over her chest, and it takes everything in me not to stare as her tits get pushed up. "Oh," she whispers.

"I can put the order into the hardware store in Mount Pleasant if you pick them up."

A smirk curves her lips. "Are you going to put them in for me too?" I nod curtly, and her expression widens. "I was just kidding. I mean, I can technically make Derek do it. You don't have to –"

I raise my eyebrows. "It's fine. Nothing I haven't done before."

Hair falls onto her cheek as she cocks her head to the side. "Were you a mechanic before you started exploring the world?"

I smile a little at that because exploring the world is putting it mildly. Very mildly. "No."

"Then how do you know how to do the spark plug thingies?"

Lifting my hand, I rub at the back of my neck, uncomfortable that we are getting dangerously close to me sharing things I'd rather not about myself. "I picked up a few things here and there."

"So, if you weren't a mechanic, what were you? And don't do that thing."

"What thing?"

She scowls at me. "That thing where you refuse to share anything with me. It drives me nuts."

I lift one eyebrow and drop my arm back to my side. "I bet it does."

"So?" She waves a hand between us. "What did you do before you started traveling?"

I debate about whether I'm going to tell her or not. Part of me wants to give in, but the other part of me knows that I can't. Instead of giving her the full truth, I say, "I made people tell the truth."

Her scowl deepens, and she takes a step closer to me. "What's that supposed to mean?"

"That's all you get to know," I rumble, looking down at her. She's so close that, if I bent at the waist, I could take her mouth like I want to. Like I *need* to.

She starts poking me in the peck and says, "That's a crap answer, and you know it." She pauses her poking before she resumes and says, "Shit, that's hard as a rock."

I snatch her hand on instinct, and she sucks in a breath at the second contact I've given her tonight. Her eyes zone in on my hand clasped around hers. My grip isn't firm, but it is commanding, and I watch as she slowly blows out her breath. She blinks, and when she reopens her eyes, I see heat there.

She raises that heat to my own gaze. Her lips part, and her

tongue slides out to gently wet them. It's almost as if she's imagining tasting me, and at that very thought, my cock stiffens slightly.

My voice is deep and husky when I say, "I can't give you the answers you're looking for, but if you want something *other* than answers, you know where to find me." Because I know for a fact it just crossed her mind.

And then I lower her hand to her side and take a step back. It's probably the hardest thing I've done in a long time, stepping away and walking away, but somehow, I manage it. She doesn't say anything at my back as I stride toward the B&B, and a part of me wishes like hell that she would just to have an excuse to bury myself inside her.

But as soon as my hand is on the knob, she calls, "Kil-lian?" It's the clear, boss-like tone again, the vulnerable woman long gone.

I turn to face her, and she doesn't fidget under my gaze even though I know she's still thinking about my offer.

Instead, she asks, "Will you go somewhere with me?"

Chapter 10

Tori Townsend

PULLING over to the side of the road, I gently place the car in Park. It idles for a moment, rumbling and vibrating me in my seat, before I turn the key, shut it off, and begin toying with my black crystal bracelet. Everything falls silent, just like the thoughts in my head. I can't help but stare to my left at that yellow dotted line that divides the traffic. That's where I hit her; that's where I ended her life.

I can sense Killian curiously glancing around from the passenger seat. I look over at him. My face is blank even though my insides feel like they're ripping apart as the entirety of guilt that I've been ignoring slams back into me.

"What is this place?" he asks, peering at the field of lilies. The raincloud may have covered up the sun, but the white petals still stand out among the green stems.

"This is where I killed someone." My tone is devoid of any emotion despite feeling them all.

His head whips my direction, and he pinches his brows

together. He looks me up and down for a second, probably seeing me in a different light. "So it was you."

"What?"

He shrugs a little. "The accident made the local news. You don't seem the murdering type."

"I'm not." I rake a hand through my hair. "At least, I wasn't."

"I don't get it," he rumbles.

Shifting slightly, I point to the road and blow out a slow breath. "I hit a pregnant woman there the other night, and she died in my arms."

He's quiet for several beats, and I don't dare look at him because what if I don't like what I see? What if I see fear? Rage? Or worse, sympathy?

"Did you know her?" he inquires quietly.

I give a small shake of my head. "No one does. The man she was running from" – I pull at my fingers until they pop – "they think she was in trouble or something. Kidnapped, probably."

Killian makes a humming sound of understanding at the back of his throat, and it's then that I chance a glance from under my lashes. He's searching the road as though he can see her ghost. I know that he won't find anything there. It's as though it never happened; the rain had washed away any evidence that anything had happened there.

He's so quiet, ever lost in thought, that I can't help but wonder what he thinks when he goes silent like this. What he holds back and what makes that secretive mind work, what makes it tick.

I don't know what it is about him, but he makes me want to learn more, to discover everything there is to know about Killian Savage. I want to know his story, and I want to know what he doesn't say and why he keeps it to himself.

Looking past him, I spot a wood bench that looks freshly

made. The wood doesn't look splintered or worn by weather yet, and on the back is an engraved gold plaque that says, 'Donated by the Wordon Family'.

I clear my throat and tip my head in that direction. "Want to sit with me?"

Before he has a chance to answer, I get out of the car and head to the bench. The ground is soft under my flip-flops, and the wet grass kisses my toes.

As soon as I take a seat, the passenger door opens and closes. For a second there, because he didn't join me right away, I didn't think he was going to come sit with me. Not that I'd blame him. I don't know him, and he certainly doesn't know me. The attraction is there though because why else would he imply that he'd screw me if I asked?

I've tried not to think about that because it would be too tempting and way too typical for me. But I get the feeling that if we did have sex, it would shift my life. Nothing would be typical about that, and I think that frightens me a little. It's probably the same reason I invited him here; because I felt some sort of connection – a different one than any friendships I currently have.

However, if he asked about sex again . . . I certainly wouldn't be capable of saying no.

He sits next to me and rests an arm on the back of the bench. We're quiet for a moment, staring out at the lilies, when he suddenly but gravely asks, "Why did you bring me here?"

I shrug a little. "Because you don't seem like the type who would overdose me with sympathy, and I didn't want to be alone when I came here."

The hum he makes again is deep and rumbly. We listen to the thunder in the distance and the birds that haven't sought shelter from the storm yet. "It gets easier," he suddenly murmurs.

I swivel my head in his direction. "What?"

His jaw clenches once, and then he's looking me dead in the eyes. "The guilt."

"Oh," I whisper. My gaze drifts across his face until it lands on his lips. "How do you know?"

"I know a lot, dollface."

My cheeks heat at the endearment, and I flick my eyes back up to his. "Care to share?"

He gives a small shake of his head, and an equally small sigh escapes me because I should have known better. "It's buried in the past, and I plan to keep it there."

My lips twist to the side, and instinctively, I scoot closer to him. If he notices, he doesn't say anything. "You must have had one hell of a life if it hurts too much to tell a stranger about it."

He cocks an eyebrow. "*Are* you a stranger?"

I try a smile at him. "I suppose not anymore. I mean, you do know a tragic thing in my life now, and you offered to fuck me, so . . ."

His chuckle is as deep as his hum had been, and the sound goes straight to my clit. It takes everything I have not to squeeze my legs shut. "What is this place? Why a field of random lilies?"

I exhale because, honestly, I don't know what he'll do with that statement, but he obviously doesn't want to talk about his past. So much so that he's switching the subject. "The flowers were planted in honor of Neil Wordon."

"I see that last name everywhere in town, and I read the article about his murder, but it didn't say anything about hundreds of flowers."

Tucking a hair behind my ear, I nod. "My best friend Tegan planted them. Everyone says she should have planted roses, but she said he'd had enough time with roses."

He turns a frown in my direction. "What's that supposed to mean?"

I wave a hand in the air. "It's a long story."

His eyebrows flick up for a second, almost as if they shrugged themselves. "My job came with certain downfalls."

My heart stutters through the next beat because I honestly hadn't expected him to share something with me after the subject change. "The getting people to tell the truth thing?"

The bun on the back of his head bobs more than his head does when he nods. The desire to let it loose and run my fingers through it is so strong that my fingers twitch. "There was a lot of death involved."

"I see," I whisper because I'm honestly too scared to say anything else. Another uttered word might frighten him off, but damn if I'm even more curious now. What the hell did he do for a living?

"Most of the time, it didn't end well. For anyone."

His face is devoid of emotion, just like mine had been in the car. I get that. Strong feelings can sometimes shut us down. "Including you?"

"Everything comes at a cost."

"Don't I know it," I murmur. Without a second thought, I grab the black crystal bracelet off my wrist and slide it onto his. "Here, you need this more than me."

"What is it?"

"A protective charm bracelet." I scowl because I had been wearing it the night of the accident. "I don't think it actually works, but it's worth a shot on someone else."

His frown is small, but he stares at the black crystals with curiosity.

Quietly, I continue, "Whatever happened to you to come this far west, I'm glad it did."

He lifts an eyebrow and turns his attention back to me. "Why?"

I shrug a little, and a ghost of a smile plays on the edges of my lips. "Because then you wouldn't have met me."

There's that deep chuckle again, and it gives me a thrill that I brought it on. He's like a treasure chest. I picked the lock, and the deeper I dig inside, the more treasures I find. "Your bossy, stubborn, sexy self?"

I blush again and look down at my lap. "Exactly." I wouldn't exactly call myself sexy. I may have been at one time, but since then, I've let myself go. Does he not see that? Or does he like his women bigger? I'm too nervous to ask him, but if I had to take a guess, I'd pick the latter one.

With the arm resting against the back of the bench, he raises his hand and twirls a finger in a loose strand of my hair. I nearly purr, and I dare not move.

"Look at me, Tori."

I glance at him from under my lashes again. "Why?"

"Because I want to see your expression when I kiss you."

I lift my chin completely, utterly shocked by his statement. He smiles at my wide eyes and slowly leans forward until his eyes close and his lips press against mine. I'm so surprised by it that I stiffen. However, his lips linger until I relax, and then he parts them and slides them along mine until I respond. I moan a little into his mouth and kiss him back, and my god, does it send electric bolts to every part of my body.

His lips are warm, and I don't know why, but he smells like cinnamon and that panty-melting, all-consuming aroma of men's soap. I didn't know I liked the scent of cinnamon until I smelled it on him. It swirls in my head, and I commit it to memory because I doubt this will ever happen again. I doubt he'll ever make another move on me and certainly not to kiss me this way.

Gently, his tongue darts out and traces the seam of my lips. I know exactly what he's asking for, and when his hand cups the back of my neck to tilt my head, I open. His tongue immediately dives inside, and I moan again because he tastes exactly as he smells. Pure. Undiluted. Powerful. Man.

I feel the kiss all the way down to my toes, and they curl against my flip-flops. It's automatic when I reach and rest my hand in the crook of his neck. The power under my fingertips is incredible, the shift of muscle when he leans a little more into the kiss.

A throat is cleared from behind us, and I pull away from the kiss. Quickly, I glance in that direction, and my soaring heart plops into the pit of my stomach when I find Pastor Kent standing there.

Chapter 11

Killian Savage

I WATCH as Tori's rosy cheeks pale, and I turn a quizzical eye on the newcomer. Underneath his orange raincoat, he's dressed in a navy blue button-down shirt and a pair of black slacks that don't have a single wrinkle in them. His black shoes shine despite the lack of sun, and each loop made in the laces is perfectly shaped. Despite how old he looks, freshly cut white hair covers his entire head, and his beard is well-cared for.

He looks back and forth between the two of us with shrewd eyes, and it's then and there that I decide that I instantly don't like the guy. I stare at him with narrowed eyes as I try to get a read on him.

After she gets over her initial shock at being caught, she squares her shoulders and juts her chin. "Pastor Kent," she greets clearly.

"I see you're making friends, Tori," he says back in a carefree tone, even though I know it's anything but.

She scowls. "I have a lot of friends."

"Sure, sure," he murmurs, and then he turns his attention to me. He holds out a hand. "Pastor Kent Hilton."

I don't shake it. I just stare at him because I made myself a promise that I'd never shake hands with a snake again.

He drops his arm back to his side when he realizes that I don't plan on introducing myself. "I haven't seen you around. You must be new to town. Are you one of Tori's 'friends'?"

I breathe deep and exhale through my nose because it's better than hitting him. "Yes," I answer. It isn't a lie. Though I may have kissed her and though we barely know each other, I've told her more about myself than I have to anyone else in a long time. That achieves friend status. Not that I'd know any different. Friends were hard to come by in my line of work.

"With benefits, I assume." His sly grin is anything but friendly.

I shrug a little and lean my side into the back of the bench. "Assume what you want."

"Oh, I don't have to truly assume anything," he says, waving a hand in the air and faking dismissal. "Tori has a reputation with men. Don't you, Tori? I'm sure you're no different."

I clench my teeth as Tori looks down at her hands folded in her lap. It takes her a moment to collect herself, to shove away the sting of his words before she raises her gaze back to his. She has a fight in her eyes as she asks, "Why are you here, Kent?"

He tips his head toward the lilies. "I came to take some lilies back to the church. The altar has been empty, and the lilies would brighten up the sanctuary."

Her eyes narrow dangerously. "They're city property. That's illegal, and you have no right to them."

His chuckle pisses me off because it's so damn arrogant. "I could argue that you have no right to seek shelter in them."

"And why is that?" I nearly growl.

The asshole keeps his gaze on Tori's glare as he answers

me. "They're a symbol of purity. With her lifestyle and her little side business, if you want to call that devil's shop a business, she doesn't fall into the category of pure. In God's eyes, she shouldn't be anywhere near them."

For a moment, my chest swells with pride because her nostrils flare, and I know that what he said may have affected her, but she wasn't going to go down without a fight. "Go to hell, Kent," she spits.

"Oh, no need." He gives her a look of sympathy. "God has preserved a space for me in heaven."

I highly doubt any sort of god would have the patience for a man like him.

"You know, the asshole who was chasing the woman I hit wore the exact same raincoat as you."

Truth be told, I've seen many people with that exact same coat. Derek probably pawned them off on customers just like he tried to do to me. But I know she was digging and probably trying to rattle him.

It doesn't seem to work.

He leans a little toward her and gives her a smile. It's almost as though he's grinning at a child for some nonsense they just said. When he doesn't seem to rattle her, he shrugs, rights himself, and heads to the lilies. From his coat pocket, he pulls out gardening shears, and as he snips his way through the flowers' stems, he says, "Funny thing about truths, they need to be backed up with proof."

My eyes narrow to little slits as I drill holes into his back with them.

With the bundle of flowers in his hand, he turns back to face us. Tori crosses her arms over her chest. "Is that what you tell your congregation?"

He begins to stride in our direction with a smirk back on his face. As soon as he passes the bench, he says, "I'm sure I'll see you both around."

As soon as he's gone, I look back at Tori, who continues to

glare in the direction he left. "You okay?" I ask, and I find that I genuinely care. It shocks me a little, but I brush it off for the moment.

She shakes herself at the sound of my voice and tucks her hair behind her ears. "He's such an asshole."

"He doesn't seem to like you." I can't imagine that many sane people would like him either.

She meets my gaze. "Yeah, he's made that plenty clear."

I tip my head slightly to the side. "Does he always antagonize you?"

Her eyebrows lower. "Any chance he gets. He's driving business away from my Wiccan shop, and he's trying to overtake my territory as a realtor."

"Hmm," I say as she looks back down at her fingers. I don't like the way she hides from me, so I reach, crook a finger under her chin, and bring her gaze back to mine. "You know I don't care that you've slept around, right?"

She laughs, but there's no humor in it. "You might be the only one. And Tegan. Kent has made a big deal about it since I slept with his grandson, and magically, everyone seems to have the same opinion."

I retuck a strand of hair that came loose. "I see no problem with the person you are."

Her forced smile fades from her face, and she searches mine for the truth. She'll find nothing otherwise there because I meant what I said. She reminds me of my past, and even though that should scare me, it doesn't at this moment. "Are you trying to get into my pants by saying nice things to me, Killian?"

I suppress my shudder at the thought of what that pretty, pink pussy looks like. Not to mention the way she said my name. I don't think she meant to, but it purred from her lips. "Are you saying you'd say no?"

Her eyes sweep my torso, and the wicked boss-lady returns. "Someone like you would have some wild kinks."

I smirk. "Someone like you has to have tried them all."

She considers me carefully again, but I note that she doesn't deny it. That's good for me because my flavor has never been vanilla. "You really don't care about being another number on my headboard?"

I lean until I'm right next to her ear and whisper, "I know that I've been dying to experience what your pussy feels like wrapped around my cock." She shivers, and I grin. "Are you sure you can handle me?"

"Maybe," she whispers back, but that one word holds so much heat that my cock hardens.

"Let's find out," I murmur, my lips tickling her ear. I pull away, and once I'm standing up, I hold out my hand for her.

"Right now?" she asks, her eyebrows high on her forehead.

I give one curt nod because, even though I don't care that I'll be a notch on her headboard, I know that she knows this will be different from the others she's slept with. I'm looking forward to showing her exactly that. And, I'm looking forward to finally quenching my thirst when it comes to all things Tori Townsend. Maybe then, my past will stop rearing its ugly head.

Chapter 12

Tori Townsend

IT WAS NOT an awkward silence on the way back home. In a husky tone, he spoke dirty things to me. Things he wanted to do, how he wanted to do them, and places he wanted to do them. I get the feeling that he's going to be more than I've ever handled, and instead of being scared, I'm even more curious. To say I was wet by the time we pulled into the driveway is an understatement. I had to bite my lip to keep from moaning out loud just by the imagery.

He didn't touch me though. He kept his hands to himself, and somehow, that made it that much more enticing. More invigorating.

With him behind me, and with the sky opening up and drenching us, I shakily try to put the key into the door. I can feel his body heat because he's standing so damn close, and it's practically a promise to all the things he told me in the car.

The keys drop from my hand onto the ground, and I curse under my breath. He chuckles and squats to grab them. But he doesn't rise. Instead, he looks up at me, and those damn eyes. They hold wicked intent.

The front of his shirt, where his jacket doesn't cover him, is as soaked as I am from the rain, and it clings to his pec muscles. Through it, I can see the distinct shape of two objects, and it's then and there that I realize his nipples are pierced. *Shit, help me.*

I meant what I said. I'm a sucker for walking red flags. For the bad boys, and he checks all the boxes that any normal person should avoid.

Droplets drip from his wet hair and down the side of his face, but he doesn't swipe them away. My chest rises and falls dramatically as he moves his gaze down my body, hovering over my pebbled nipples, which are definitely visible through my soaked shirt, and all the way down until they land on the hem of my sweatpants.

The way he stares makes goosebumps rise over my skin, and it has nothing to do with the rain. It's like he's guessing at what treasure he'll find inside. With one hand, he reaches, tucks a finger under the hem, and skims just above my pussy.

My damn legs tremble, and he knows it because a smirk takes over that damn sexy mouth.

He dips his hand a little lower, over the hill of my pubic bone, and grazes my clit. I suck in a sharp breath and jerk because, honestly, it's been a long damn time since someone has touched it. And to have Killian touch it? Soaking wet? Smelling of cinnamon and man and rain?

Fuck, don't fall apart before we even step foot inside.

A crack of lightning brightens our space, and a rumble of thunder hides my brief whimper. He slides his finger over my clit again, and I brace myself by grasping his shoulder.

"Oh my god," I whisper on my next breath. The rain pelting us carries away my next unintelligible plea.

He makes a humming noise at the back of his throat, stuffs the keys into his jacket pocket, and lowers my sweatpants. I stand there naked from my hips down with my sweatpants pooled around my flip-flops, desperately wondering what the hell he has planned next.

Carefully, as though he doesn't want to tip me over, he grasps my ankle, lifts it, and pulls my sweatpants off from around it while removing one of my flip-flops at the same time. He does the same with the other and then drops the pants next to the door. It's on the tip of my tongue, the desire to ask him what he's doing and to remind him that there are people who could probably see out of their back windows, our backyards touching, but my words are cut off when he takes my knee and puts it over his shoulder.

"Such a pretty fucking pussy," he rumbles.

I shudder when he presses a kiss to my pussy, and as he gently bites my throbbing clit, I tip my head back and let the rain shower my face. I no longer care if people see what he's doing to me. I don't give a shit about the rain or the possibility of being struck by lightning. All the fuck I care about is that he makes me cum. Right here. Right now.

I tip my head back down and look at his head buried between my thighs. His free hand rides up the back of my leg that's holding me up until he cups my ass to keep me from swaying away from him. The sight of him between my legs, the feel of his five o'clock stubble, and the tickle of his bun is almost too much to handle. It sends sensations all over my body.

His tongue flicks out and lazily slides along my clit. His moan can be felt across my entire body, and my breathing picks up pace. I squeeze his shoulder and bury my nails into the leather of his jacket because… *Oh. My. God.*

I push my pussy further into his face, and he chuckles against me. "So damn greedy." His eyes flick up to mine, and they contain such heat that I bite my bottom lip to keep from falling apart before he's even finished. "Do you need to cum, dollface?"

I whimper and nod.

"Beg."

"W-what?"

The hand holding my thigh over his shoulder reaches underneath and drags along the length of my clit. "Beg for it."

My lips part because it's completely against my nature to beg for anything. I've done it before with my ex but for other things like love and affection, and I told myself I'd never do it again. But here we are, me and Killian, and he's asking me to plead my case to get what I want.

Can I do it? Can I utter the words for the man that has completely captured my interest?

I just can't help myself when I murmur heatedly, "Please, Killian." I sob out of desperation because I know that everything he promised me in the car will be wilder than my imagination dreamed up. "Please make me cum."

His groan is my first reward, and without tearing his gaze from me, he sucks my clit into his mouth as the prize. "Holy shit," I whisper as I buck against him.

As he sucks, he flicks his tongue against the tight bud, and my legs quake so hard that it's a miracle I'm still standing. Yet, his one hand is keeping me up, a firm grip against me. His fingers dig into the soft flesh, a bite of pain that I hadn't expected to like. All my other lovers have been gentle, so my eyes widen in surprise as my lower abdomen clenches, betraying the fact that I just might actually like it.

I suck in a sharp breath when he scrapes his teeth against my clit and groan when he soothes it with a swipe of his tongue. He returns to pulling on my clit, a sucking motion that times with the rapid beat of my heart. Whimpers leave the back of my throat, my pussy pulses, and my thigh tightens around his head. The fire in my lower abdomen begins, and electric shocks zip from what he's doing to my clit all the way up to my impossibly tight nipples.

A few more zaps and I groan so deep as I cum that it

sounds like the thunder above us. I rock against his face, and he rides it out, sucking and flicking until I sag against the hand that's holding me up.

He chuckles, lowers my leg from his shoulder, and rises. His face glistens with more than rain, evidence of what he just did to me. Out in the open. Under a storm.

His lips gently take my own, forcing me to taste myself, and I don't hate it. His tongue is sweet as it dives into my mouth, and for a moment there, we kiss desperately.

When he pulls away, he asks, "Are you ready, Tori?" And I get the feeling that he's asking if I can handle him again.

I bite my bottom lip and nod because there's no way I'm backing out now.

Taking the keys from his pocket, he unlocks the door, grabs my hand, and leads me inside. I step over my soaked sweatpants and into the warmth of the house. The mud from my bare feet leaves tracks against the floor as we hurriedly walk through the kitchen and dining room.

"Bedroom?" he asks huskily.

"Down the hall."

He guides us down the dark hallway that's lit briefly by another crack of lightning. Once we're inside, I move to flick on the lights, but he stops me with a hand on the back of mine.

I lift an eyebrow at him, but he nods in the direction of the lamp that's squatting on the nightstand beside my bed. He lets go of my hand and crosses the bedroom to it. With a twist of his wrist, he dimly lights the room.

And then he turns to me, slides off his jacket, and drops it to the floor. For some odd reason, the wet plop it makes makes my pussy clench. Slowly, he grabs the hem of his shirt and lifts the dripping-wet garment over his head.

My lips part as I take him in.

Pure, godly, gorgeousness.

His muscles shift and ripple as he drops the shirt onto his

jacket. Dark tattoos cover every inch of his thick arms, defined pecs, and the bumps of his abs. Every inch of him glistens from the rain, and I can't believe that, in moments, this man will be driving into me.

I was right about the nipple piercings too. The studs shine in the dim light.

I lower my gaze to the bulge that presses against his jeans, which stick to him like a second skin. I can't help the gulp.

"Tori," he calls in a deep tone.

I flick my eyes back to his. "Hmm?"

"Take off your clothes."

Even though I have body issues, I do as he asks because, by his expression, he wants to see me naked. He wants to take it all in like I took him in, and that tells me he finds me attractive even if I don't.

It takes some strength, but I manage to get my shirt over my head. I pull off my bra next, and he hums his approval at what he sees. His hands flex at his sides like he wants to cross the room and touch me, but his eyes raking over my naked body is touch enough.

"I'm going to fucking destroy you," he whispers.

I suppress the moan.

"What do you have for toys?" he asks.

"W-what?"

He looks back at my eyes again. "I like certain things. I want to see if you can meet those needs."

I twist my lips to the side and then whisper, "Nightstand."

He turns to the nightstand, and I get the full of his muscular back. Tattoos cover his skin here too, and I don't have time to study them because he's pulling things out of my nightstand and setting them on the bed.

A condom and fuzzy pink handcuffs first and then one of the things I've never used but bought as a joke: nipple clamps. And lastly, he pulls out the knife I keep there for protection. It's large and curved and has a big, thick wooden handle. I don't like guns, and Cole had bought it for me when I moved into this house. Tegan didn't like that I was alone, and Cole, knowing his wife was worried, picked it up at the thrift store. It was my housewarming gift. An odd one but one that's helped me peacefully sleep alone at night.

I approach the bed with a frown. "You want to use these on me?" I ask as I pick up the nipple clamps.

He shuts the nightstand drawer, turns back toward me, and takes my chin. Gently, he kisses me. "They're for me," he whispers against my lips.

My eyebrows fly into my forehead. "I've-"

He kisses me again, silencing me, and says, "I like pain, dollface. Still think you can handle me?"

And then it all makes sense. The nipple piercings, his body covered in tattoos. He enjoyed the pain. A nervousness curls in my gut. I've never delivered pain. Ever since I moved here, my other lovers have been too vanilla. They never ventured far into the realm of possibilities even when I asked based on my own fantasies and desires.

When he said that I seemed the type to have 'tried them all', he was wrong. I've only dreamed about them.

So, I ask myself again, can I do this? Can I give him what he needs?

I have no idea, but I sure as shit am going to try.

My nod is small as I bite my bottom lip. He smirks and lets go of my face to lower the zipper of his jeans. I can't help it. I have to watch. Slowly, almost as if he wants me to take in everything and not miss a second of it, he pushes his jeans and briefs over his ass and down his knees.

His cock glistens from dampness in what little light we have, and it's larger than the earlier bulge teased at. He gives me a second to stare before he slides all the way out of his jeans, revealing more tattoos along his legs. Next, he bites the condom wrapper, opens it, and puts it on his length. Once he's wrapped, he picks up the handcuffs and dangles them between us.

"Last chance."

My only answer is confidently taking the handcuffs from him. His smile is wide, and then he's crawling onto the bed, giving me a perfect view of that full, muscular ass. He flips over, lays on his back, and connects his wrists.

I gulp again as he looks at me expectantly. Careful to avoid the sharp blade of the knife, I climb onto the bed with him. As soon as I reach him, I fasten his wrists to the headboard and then sit back on my knees and take him all in again.

I like the sight I see, him lying there, tied up and at my mercy, waiting for pain and pleasure.

Glancing over, I pick up the nipple clamps. In seconds, and surprisingly confidently, I fasten them to his nipples. His eyes close against the pain, pure and utter bliss. I squeeze my thighs together as my pussy clenches.

With no plan in mind, I grab the knife and straddle him, one leg on either side and hovering the tip of his cock at my entrance. His eyes open, half-hooded and full of lust. It urges me on. I take his cock with my free hand and sink down onto him. We groan together, the stretch so delicious to accommodate his size.

"So. Fucking. Tight," he growls through clenched teeth.

My eyelids flutter in bliss. I rock against him at the same time I tug on the chain connecting his nipple clamps. His head digs into the pillow as he throws it back and moans. It makes me feel powerful, and as I rock again, I bring the knife up and study the blade. It could do some serious damage if I'm not careful.

"Do it," he demands, and I look at him to find him staring at me.

The trust he has in me is more than I have in myself. But instead of thinking too hard about it, I continue to rock along his cock, moaning at the feel of him, and press the edge of the blade to the space above his navel.

And then I press and drag it.

As blood wells, he sucks in a breath and moans so deep that it vibrates his cock. It twitches inside me, and my own moan matches his. And damn it if it doesn't urge me on.

An inch above the first cut, I press and drag again. His wrists strain against the cuffs, and his fingers flex and unflex.

"Did I hurt you?" I ask, unsure as I continue to ride him.

"Fuck no," he mutters so deeply. "Again."

Droplets of blood spread across his abs and drip onto my comforter, but I do as he asks and slice into him again. None of my cuts are deep enough for stitches, but they're enough that he's a moaning, godly mess. Slick with blood. Slick with sweat. It makes my pussy clench and milk his length. I can feel his thighs ripple with strain, and with a quick glance, I watch as his toes curl.

Fucking hot.

I shouldn't like this. I should be terrified of this, of him. But god damn it, I'm not. This is the hottest thing I've ever seen, this man at my mercy, this man begging in heated whispers beneath me for more while I ride him.

On my next slice, he bucks into me, juts his chin toward the ceiling, and buries himself so deep that I practically see stars. It's enough to make me scream a surprise orgasm. I ride him faster, harder, chasing myself straight into a heaven I don't believe in. I drop the knife and grasp his bloody and slick waist, riding him greedily.

"Fuck," he hisses. "Shit." The chain of the cuff rattles, and the headboard groans as he tugs on the cuffs. He rears a little off the pillow, parts his lips as he watches my pussy swallow him, and his eyes widen as he cums. His cock pulses inside me as he fills the condom, and the swell of his dick sends me over the edge again. I tip my head back and scream with the all-consuming release. The orgasm reaches every part of my body, a fiery inferno, and it takes everything I have to keep breathing.

It subsides, and he finishes at the same time I do. He flops back onto the pillow, out of breath and his eyes closed in post-sex bliss.

"Holy shit," I breathe on a heavy exhale.

He hums at the back of his throat and opens his eyes, scanning his body and then mine. I do so too, examining the cuts and then the blood all over my hands.

"Untie me," he whispers.

I climb off of him, grab the keys from the nightstand, and stick them into the cuff's holes. Once his wrists are free and the nipple clamps removed, he grabs my face and kisses me with such passion that I practically melt against him.

"We made a mess," I murmur against him.

He smiles as he pulls away. "Do you have a towel you don't care about?"

"All my towels are black," I say. I climb off the bed, head out into the hallway, and grab a towel from the linen closet. I come back to him, and he moves to take the towel from me, but I hold it close to my chest and shake my head. "Let me."

He considers me carefully before propping himself up on his elbows. Gently, I swipe away the blood while he watches. While I do so, I ask, "Why do you like pain?" Because there has to be a reason, right?

His shrug is small, and I know that's the only answer I'm going to get. I have a feeling it's part of the mystery that is Killian Savage. As I toss the towel into the hamper, I decide that I like the mystery. That I like him, and that I hope to god this isn't the last time I experience this with him.

Chapter 13

Tori Townsend

“I GET the feeling you don’t like birthdays very much,” I say to Josiah with my lips thinned. He is just about done with his shift, Tegan having just arrived to replace him, but he’s helping her restock. We’ve told him Happy Birthday twice now, and he doesn’t seem too thrilled about this milestone age. Tegan even brought him a homemade cake, and he mumbled his, “Thank you.”

“Yeah, kid. You’re a man now,” Tegan claims, dropping the small box she was carrying and giving him a little shake on the shoulders.

He grins, but it doesn’t reach his eyes. “Age doesn’t make you a man,” he explains.

I cock my head to the side while grabbing another empty box and preparing to set it by the back door to be taken out. “Then what makes a person a man if it’s not age?”

He glances at me with a true smile and sparkling eyes. “How they deal with the biggest change in their life.”

Tegan cocks her head to the side too, pausing in ripping open the box. "And that is?"

He shrugs a little and sets a book on the shelf for display. "It could be many things, but I believe the truth is told when they have a child. A lot of men aren't really men until they step up to the plate as a father."

I scowl because, though he's not right, he's also not wrong. It makes me wonder if he's observing this from his father's behavior, whether that be a good thing or a bad thing. Or it could simply be an observation of the world. "Fair point," I eventually say, taking the empty box from before his feet and bringing it to the back as well. I check the clock on the way back. "Anyway, you should get going. Your shift is well over."

He nods, sets another book on the shelf, and then dusts his hands together. I don't miss the puppy-dog eyes when he turns in my direction and meets my gaze. "See you tomorrow?"

"Sure, kid." Satisfied, he strides to the door and walks out gracefully. I watch through the windows as he moves down the sidewalk to wherever he parked his car today. When he's gone, I turn to Tegan. "He's an odd one."

She holds up a finger. "But he's hard-working."

"True."

"It also helps that I'm eighty percent sure his crush on you is his biggest motivator."

I roll my eyes and grab the now-empty box in front of her. "Do you believe what he said? About a man being a man when he steps up to the plate when he has a child?"

"I mean . . ." I turn to face her and see an expression on her face that I don't normally see. Guilt. Uncertainty. "Yeah," she adds.

I narrow my eyes. "I see Cole as a man, and he doesn't have a child." Hell, even Killian is a man. I fully believe that whatever past he had made him into one – to know what he wants, to be the sort of personality he is. He's seen things,

things that took him from a boy into a man. I have no doubt in my mind.

She grabs her fingers and starts to twist them. "About that-"

I tense. "Don't tell me Cole has a baby somewhere."

Slowly, she meets my gaze. "Not yet, no."

I scowl again. "What do you mean?" My eyes widen. "Did he cheat on you? Oh my god, he got her pregnant. I'm going to kill him!" I make to move to the door to do just that, but her next words stop me.

"It's me. I'm the pregnant one, Tori," she sighs out.

I freeze and whip back to face her. Her hands are covering her lower abdomen, and a growing smile crosses her face. "Holy shit," I whisper as excitement starts to bubble up inside me. "You're pregnant?"

She nods.

Squealing, I head to her and wrap her in a hug. "This is so great!" I bounce her a little, and she laughs into my ear. When I pull away, I ask, "How far along are you?"

"I just finished the first trimester."

I look down at her stomach and see a slight bulge. My own feelings of guilt punch me in the gut. "How did I not notice?"

"Well," she begins, chuckling a little. "We have been eating a lot of donuts."

Her words do nothing to sway my guilt. "I should have noticed something like this."

She only shrugs. "You've had a lot going on. Between your two businesses and, you know . . . the accident, it's a wonder you haven't broken down yet."

I dutifully ignore the accident part because, if I let it register with me, I'll see that woman's eyes again. Instead, I shake myself a little, almost like a shiver, and shove all my feelings aside because this is her moment. Not mine. "Do you know what you're having yet?"

"No, we won't know that for a while, but I don't think we want to find out. I do, however, know who the godmother is."

She stares at me long and hard, and then it hits me. I point to myself and ask, "Me?" A little bit of panic rings in my voice.

She blinks at me hard and groans. "I know you don't want kids and that they terrify you. And I know that if Cole and I die, that means you're the caretaker of the kid, but the chances of that happening are so slim they shouldn't even be on your radar."

A sliver of relief fills me. Not wanting kids is an understatement. I'll never change my mind on that. While I get that some people can't live without the idea of having a growing family, that's never been something I've ever wanted. Kids scare me. Being a mother scares me. Being responsible for anyone but myself scares me. I've always been this way, and I like the life I have now, even if it does get a little lonely.

"So what do I do then? As a Godmother?"

She shrugs, but I can tell that she's relieved that I didn't go into full-blown panic on her. "Spoil them."

I place my hands on my hips. "Like candy and gifts and such?"

"Exactly." She picks up the last box, opens it, and places the crystals on the shelf. When she's finished, she hands it to me. She looks at me thoughtfully as I take it from her. "I know you don't want a family, but have you thought about a husband?"

I shake my head and back up a step. "No husband. Maybe a life partner, but there's no way I'm signing a legal document tying me to someone else for the rest of my life."

A sly smile takes over her face. "Not even someone like Killian?" I blush and glance away, and this only causes her to laugh. "I knew it. What's going on between you and your tenant?"

I turn my attention to my shoes and cringe. "We, uh . . . we had sex."

She doesn't say anything for a moment, so I look up and watch as she blinks dumbfoundedly. "I wasn't aware you guys were even on full talking terms, let alone 'under the sheets' terms."

"It just kind of happened."

"Which part? The sex or the friendly part?"

I cringe again. "Both."

She shakes her head like she just can't believe me, but she should have known better. I am who I am. Dick is an essential food group of mine. "Well, how was it?"

I wet my bottom lip as I think back to last night. He hung around for a good hour, asking me about my life, before he left and went back to the B&B to sleep. I had expected him to leave right away, not to ask me personal questions. He doesn't seem the type for idle conversation, but maybe he didn't want to be alone as much as I didn't want to be last night and needed excuses to stay. However, today I keep replaying our time together – the sex – and how different it'd been than my past lovers. And how much I liked it – watching him squirm with the need for pain and pleasure… I've never seen nor been a part of something like that in my life.

"He's kinky," I say in a way of explanation.

"Like?" she presses with a raise of her eyebrows.

I only lift a shoulder and let it fall lazily. "He likes pain."

She blinks hard. "I – Well – I mean, okay."

"That's all you have to say about it?"

She holds up her hands. "Hey, I'm not one to judge. I like to fear not breathing; Cole likes to choke me; you like cock; he likes pain. We all have our things."

I chuckle at that because she's not wrong.

"What about Pierce?" She whispered his name like it was a secret.

"What about him?"

"You know . . ."

I chuff when I understand her question. "I'm not his property, and he has no claim to me. He can think whatever he wants."

"If you say so," she sing-songs. "But I guarantee you, if he finds out about you and Killian, he'll get territorial."

She's not wrong about that either. I honestly don't know what I can do to get the guy to realize that there is absolutely nothing between the two of us and there will never be.

My alarm goes off on my phone, and I move the box to the other hand to grab it out of my back pocket. "I have to go. Derek is meeting me downtown."

"Okay." She places her hands on her hips and blows her hair out of her face. "Do you want me to take out the boxes?"

I shake my head. No way am I having a pregnant chick do manual labor. If I had known sooner, she wouldn't have been picking up any boxes today. "There's only a couple. I just take them out real quick."

She nods, and I head to the back of the shop, awkwardly gather the boxes in my arms, and use my foot to kick open the back door. Once outside, I sigh when sprinkles peck my cheeks because I don't know how much more rain I can handle.

I travel down the alley, lost in thought about the one and only Killian Savage and how I'm just now noticing that he didn't offer up anything about himself last night, that I almost missed the sensation. That tingly awareness. That prickle on the back of the neck. The one that tells me that I'm being watched.

Slowing my steps feet from the dumpster, I carefully swivel around with my boxes. All I see is an empty entrance. No one is there, but the feeling doesn't go away. "Calm down, Tori," I murmur to myself, walking backward the rest of the way to the dumpster.

Tires squeal at the opposite end of the alley, causing me to jump and the boxes to fly from my hands. I whip back around, but the car is gone before I can get a glimpse of it.

Heart in my throat, I quickly throw away the boxes and dash my way back inside.

I STEP out of the empty downtown building and suck in fresh air. Even though it's raining, it's a far better smell than the dust and mildew stench from inside. It didn't take long for Derek to say he'd buy it, however, despite the state of the interior. Lord knows what he plans to do with this place, but whatever it is, it'll probably be a need of the community and therefore popular like all of his other businesses.

No doubt, Cole will be the one to fix this place up.

Stepping to my right, I yank the red 'For Sale' sign off of the window, and as I crumple it up in my hands, I look around at my surroundings, still shaken from the alleyway. The whole way back to Fairview, I glanced in my mirror, but I was never followed. I was alone on the road for the most part, and yet, I still couldn't shake the feeling that someone had been watching me.

Now, as I look around, people pay me no attention. It's enough to satisfy my need for safety, and as I go to throw the sign in the nearby city trash, I pause. Walking around the corner is a couple, and they're both wearing orange raincoats. My blood quickens in my veins, and I work hard to keep my breathing even as the memories of that night surface.

The door to the building opens, and Derek steps outside with a little cough and picks up the umbrella he left by the doorway. "Dusty," he explains as he clears his throat.

"Huh?" I answer as I watch the couple walk past us.

He comes to stand beside me, eyeing me with curiosity before following my line of sight. "Know them?"

I shake my head. "No. But the coats…"

"Ah yes," he says with a prideful puff of his chest. He

opens his umbrella and holds it over his head. My wet hair and I glare at it as he adds, "They're selling well. I'll have to order more if this rain continues."

"Well, you sold a coat to someone who was kidnapping or something."

He turns a frown in my direction. "So I've been told. I can't help who buys from me."

Wet hair clings to my face, so I shove it away irritably with the dire desire to snap at him for purchasing so many that everyone now has one. They're practically a fashion movement. "I know," I all but spit.

He studies me for a moment. "How are you holding up?"

"I wish everyone would stop asking me that," I grumble under my breath.

"You have a lot of people who care about you, Tori."

I blow out an exhale. "Yeah, I know."

"Are you at least talking to someone about it?"

"Yeah, I have someone." *More like fucking him, but that's beside the point.* He listened to me, didn't give me an overwhelming amount of sympathy, and instead, gave me exactly what I needed. On some level, I knew he understood. It was written all over his face on the bench by the lilies.

Derek opens his mouth to say something else, probably some advice from the heart, but I step away from him and point to the sky and the rain that pelts us. "I should go."

"Right," he whispers, his face pinched in confusion. "Call me when you complete the paperwork?"

I nod, say my farewell, and dash to my borrowed car. Once I get inside, I rest my forehead against the steering wheel and work to calm the memories that threaten to choke me.

Chapter 14

Killian Savage

SOFT COUNTRY MUSIC plays over the speakers at the gas station. I've never been a fan of the genre, but this particular song is 'okay'. I'm more of a blues fan, and the more cities and towns I travel through, the more I realize that the genre is hard to come by.

I snap the bracelet Tori gave to me in time with the music as I search the frosty fridges for tonight's dinner. I have the urge to cook something, but here, where the options are limited to sandwiches, wraps, pizza, and a various array of junk food, my choices are limited to none.

Before, I used to cook all the time. Nice meals for *her*. For one of the persons who meant the world to me. Cooking had always been a way to escape my job, a task to make a few simple and ordinary ingredients into something that was bright and delicious and not so dark and daunting as my life was.

Now…now it's always dark. Now, I'm looking for meals to microwave, the past me almost gone yet trying to resurface in a gas station in the middle of Nowhere, Utah. I snap the bracelet against my wrist again as I stand in front of the pizzas, contemplating the reason that I have this urge to bring a part of myself back. Hell, even the urge to stay a little longer in Fairview than I had originally planned.

I avoid the topic in my thoughts, but I know it's because of a particular woman. The woman who reminds me of *her.* With Tori around, it's like *she's* still with me. I don't know if it makes me sane or insane for practically needing Tori for me to feel like I can breathe again. To feel like there's hope for me beyond my vengeance for this man who took everything from me in a single night. For a man who has to know that I'm coming for him. Why else would he disappear?

Bringing the bracelet up to my nose, I take a subtle whiff. It still has a faint, delicate scent of perfume on it, something Tori hasn't worn around me yet. I like the smell, but I prefer her own unique scent that's close to the lilies in the field that were witness to our first connection. The connection where she told me she killed someone.

It's wrong of me to feel closer to her for that than I have with anyone else since I was recruited into my past job? Killing sometimes happened. It was a hazard of the job… and the first time? That was the worst of them all. I don't know if I'm qualified to help her through this, and I don't even know if I can, but I do know that it makes me feel something for her. A deeper connection than the trust in the confession.

A part of me wants to avoid it, avoid her, but the other part of me knows that might be impossible.

I open the fridge and grab a cold cheeseburger, frustrated with myself that I'm deterring from my purpose. I should take the bracelet off and hand it back to her, but I don't think I have it in me to just . . . end whatever this is. I know it has to end at some point, yes. I'm not stupid. However, I am greedy, and that greed is the only thing stopping me. Greed for her. Greed for a sliver of what I once had.

Browsing the chip aisle, I ignore the ding of the gas station's doorbell like I've been ignoring the tune the cashier has been playing by tapping against the counter while she waits for me to make my choices.

When this person stops beside me though, I pretend not to notice because he's wearing a certain uniform that I try to avoid. I can feel his glances at me while he pretends to look at the chips with me, so it's no surprise when he asks, "You Killian Savage?"

I get a glimpse of him – short black hair, clean-shaven face, kind eyes – before I respond with, "Does it matter?"

I don't know how he knows my name, but I find that I don't like that he does. It makes me wonder what else he knows about me.

He picks up a bag of chips and looks at the back as if he cares about the ingredients. Anyone getting chips couldn't care less about what's inside them. No. He's pretending to care so that he has a reason to talk to me, and therefore, that means this is a purposeful visit.

"I'll take that as a yes," he murmurs.

"Take it however you want."

He places the bag back on the shelf and turns to face me. "I'm Pierce Hilton, the Sheriff."

"Lucky you."

Crossing his arms, he presses on. "Why are you here, Killian?"

Without looking at him, I raise my wrapped cheeseburger. "Food."

He readjusts his arms as if my answer made him uncomfortable. We both know that wasn't the question he was asking. "I meant in Fairview."

"Just passing through," is all I rumble.

"People like you don't just pass through."

Narrowing my eyes, I finally turn to face him. He's shorter

than I am, less built, but I give him credit because he doesn't cower. "People like me?"

His eyes sweep my body before they return to mine. "I know trouble when I see it."

"Who said I was looking for trouble?"

He matches my expression, and I know he's not going to back down until he gets his point across. "I looked into you, Killian. I know just about everything there is to know about Killian Savage. Well, almost everything. I still have some unanswered questions. Was hoping you could help me out with that."

My nostrils flare, and I push past him, saying, "This conversation is over."

The cashier watches warily as I place my sandwich on the counter, dig in my pocket for cash, and quickly pay her. "Keep the change," I mutter, and then I'm out the door.

"I know everything you've done. Everything you've lost. I can even guess at why you're just 'passing through,'" Pierce says as he follows me past the gas pumps.

"Then I suppose that's enough to leave me alone," I grumble over my shoulder.

I hear him stop in his tracks, and he starts listing names. Names I'm familiar with. Names I've tried hard to forget because they're part of my life better left whispered into the abyss. It's enough to make me stop, however. "All people you worked for," he adds when I don't make a move to continue toward the sidewalk. "All people with deep pockets and a criminal list so long that law enforcement can't even put a finger on them."

"And how would you know that?" I ask, my heart beating fast. He knows more than I thought he would. Too much, in fact. I turn to face him once more.

His eyebrows are raised. "Because I was a cop in New York once. I know exactly who the people are that employed you."

Angrily, I slice an arm through the air. "My purpose for passing through has nothing to do with them. That was my past. That isn't my present."

A beat passes where he says nothing, but then he takes a few steps closer in my direction. "Pasts have a funny way of following us, no matter how far we run. I don't fully know what you're chasing, but I guarantee you that it has everything to do with your past. You're looking for something, and I have half a mind to believe it has to do with your employers."

"It doesn't." The words were bit out through clenched teeth.

"Forgive me if I don't believe you."

I turn on my heel and make my way to the sidewalk, absolutely done with this conversation. I've done nothing wrong here, and all he has is guesses. He has nothing to nail me with. He doesn't even know what I did for those people. If he did, I'd be arrested by now.

"I will find out, Killian!" he shouts at my back, still rooted in the spot I left him.

"Good luck with that," I shout back because I was careful back then. I'm still careful now, but my past? I knew how to hide my tracks. I knew how to be invisible until called upon by the snakes that employed me to do their dirty work. He'll find nothing to put me away for.

Chapter 15

Tori Townsend

RAIN. *It's always the rain.*

I'm being pelted with it while I walk down the road, balancing on the yellow, faded centerline. The rain is cold against my skin, and the breeze that comes with the night air is chilly. It's an all-too-familiar scene, this road. This weather. This area.

I stop in my tracks, letting the droplets drip into my eyes and blur my vision. Why am I here? It seems so . . . I glance at the road and watch as dark blood mixes with the flow of rain that drains down the side of the pavement. It touches my bare feet, mixing in the space between my toes.

My breath catches in my throat, and I start to hop back, but movement to my right makes me swiftly turn. A woman stands there, and everything comes crashing back. That night. That crash. Her dead eyes. But at this moment, her dead eyes are very much alive. The woman I hit stands there with the lilies as her background. Even though I feel fear, I slowly make my way toward her, off the road, past the bench, and all the way until I stand before her.

I shake, knees knocking together, and it has nothing to do with the chill.

The rain doesn't seem to affect her. It's as though it parts just for her. Her hair isn't wet. Her clothes are not soaked. The bottom of her dress doesn't blow with the breeze, but the middle of her dress pulls tight around her swollen belly.

Blood drips from her nose, however, cascading around the hills of her lips to race toward her chin. She opens her mouth to say something, her teeth covered in blood, but no words come out.

"I can't hear you," I say above the pelting rain. She mouths something again, and I frown. "What?"

Sorrow takes over her face, and her lips pull downward in disappointment. She looks at her hand by her side and then lifts her arm. Once it's in front of me, she turns her wrist and points to the brand there, that of a lily that mimics the shadows of those behind her.

And then she collapses to the ground, a heap of the mess I found her in when I hit her – limbs twisted in the wrong direction, gaze on the flowers.

A fresh wave of fear grips me, and I drop to my knees, quietly begging her to stay alive.

I JOLT awake and gasp for air. Papers fly from my chest and flutter to the ground, and because of the blood rushing through my ears, it takes me a moment to realize where I am.

My dark living room comes into view as goosebumps rise over my skin. The dream felt so real. The rain, the cold, and the intense emotions. I thought I had been doing a good job ignoring the fact of what I did, but my subconscious rears its ugly head and makes me relive the scariest parts of it.

Slowly, I sit up on the couch and run a hand through my hair. The lamp on the end table beside me casts a soft glow around the living room, aiding me in getting a grip on my surroundings.

"It was just a dream," I whisper shakily to myself. "Just a dream."

I tap my cheeks to get feeling back into them and lean over

the couch to pick up the papers I had dropped. I didn't mean to fall asleep getting the paperwork together for Derek, but I must have been exhausted, closed my eyes for a second, and drifted off.

Leafing through the mess in my hands, I re-order them and straighten the stack on my knee. Nowadays, the paperwork is handled electronically, but Derek is old-fashioned and likes it all to be on physical copies. It makes more work for me, but I honestly don't mind. His business is keeping a roof over my head.

A prickly sensation begins at the back of my neck, just like the one I felt when I was in the alley. This time, I listen to it right away and freeze. With a quick swivel of my eyes, I glance around the room. Aside from the furniture, I'm alone, but that doesn't make me breathe easier. I'm being watched . . . but from where?

I flick my attention to the TV on the wall. Even though it's dark, it reflects the view outside my big window. Fear, just like that of my dream, spikes in my veins when I see an orange blob amid the darkness. It may be blurry from the warped reflection, but I've seen that raincoat enough to recognize it even in a distorted state.

Though I don't want to, even though everything screams in me not to, I turn my head toward the window. The tall bush-like trees sway before my vision falls solely on what I'm searching for, and a blur of orange leaves the window.

Papers flying once again to the ground, I leap off the couch because, even if I didn't see an actual person, I know one was there. I stand there for a moment, eyes searching the darkness while every pore on my body is prickling with awareness.

That person had to have been tall, based on how high my window is and the height of the blob in my TV. I can think of only one person who is that tall and also owns one of those raincoats. There's also only one person I know who would have the audacity to spy on me too, who hates me enough to do so.

"Kent," I breathe out.

I head to the window, a fresh wave of fear and added anger gripping me. Not only was he watching me while I was vulnerable, but the entire thing felt predatorial. I don't like to be scared in my own home, and he just took my safety from me in a matter of seconds. How long was he watching me? Why was he watching me? What did he plan to do?

I search outside my window, but I see nothing but darkness and wet road. Either he took off faster than I could get my wits about me, or he's still hanging around.

Whipping back around, I snatch my phone off the end table and stand there for a moment, debating about who to call. Do I call Tegan? It's late, and she could be in bed. I don't want to disturb her sleep. I could call Cole and ask him to stop over and make sure I'm truly alone now, but that could wake up Tegan too.

I glance at the back door, the one that leads to the backyard and the B&B that squats in it. Do I dare call Killian? No. No, I can't make my problem his problem.

Just as I'm about to dial 9-1-1, a knock sounds at my door, causing me to jump. My phone tumbles to the ground on top of the dropped papers, and my hand flies to my chest. I stare at the front door, teeth gritted in terror. Would Pastor Kent knock on my door? The stupid thing would be to answer it. That's how I'd die, I just know it.

I whirl, about to dash to my bedroom to grab the knife Cole gave me, but a voice outside my front door stops me. "Tori!" Pierce calls. "I know it's late, but please open up."

I breathe a sigh of relief, stride to my door, and open it. My relief quickly fades when I see him standing there, and not alone. Behind him are two other cops.

Frowning, I take in his expression. It's hard, not the usual sweet expression that I've come to associate him with. "Pierce?" I cross my arms over my chest as the chill from the damp night filters into my house. Whatever this is, it isn't a social call, and any idea of telling him that his grandfather just watched me outside my window flees from my mind. "What's going on?"

Pierce stuffs his hands into his pockets. "Sorry to wake you," he says.

My frown only deepens. "It's fine," I answer, and then I ask again, "What's going on? Am I in some sort of trouble?"

I wouldn't put it past someone like Pastor Kent to make up some kind of lie to get me arrested. He's basically done everything else to make me the black sheep of the town.

He shakes his head and glances around for a second. Then, he sighs. "Someone has been kidnapped."

"Oh my god," I breathe. That was the last thing I expected him to say. "Who?"

"Susan Toro."

"Oh my god," I breathe again. I don't know her well, but she has stopped into my shop a few times. She's one of those people who are superstitious and come in for charms to turn around her luck. She's been trying to get her sewing business going, but it hasn't been going well.

I saw her just the other day, in fact, walking around the shops in Mount Pleasant. We had waved at each other, but I did note the stress that lined her face. As a single woman trying to make it on her own, I brushed it off as money worries. She has mentioned that before, so it was the obvious conclusion. But to know that she's been kidnapped? I can't even imagine what she's going through right now.

"Yeah," he says on an exhale, and for a moment, stress wrinkles his forehead.

"By who?"

His lips twist to the side for a moment, almost as though he's considering whether or not to tell me. "We don't know, but a witness says by a man in an orange raincoat and a black van."

Tonight is the night of fear because it grips me so tight this time that nausea builds inside my stomach. I snatch a hand up to grip that section of my abdomen, trying like hell not to hurl on his shoes.

"When?" I whisper.

"Early evening," he answers.

I manage to nod as my mind races. "Why are you telling me all this?"

He glances back at the cops behind him and then looks back at me again. "Is Killian Savage in the B&B?"

"He's never in, but . . ." I blink a few times and then scowl. What kind of trouble does Killian get into when he's gone? And what the hell does it have to do with this visit? "Probably is now, why?"

"I'm sorry to do this, Tori, however . . ." He takes a folded paper out of his back pocket and passes it to me. "This is a warrant to search the B&B and Killian's belongings."

"What?" I screech as he and the others start to take off toward the side of my house and bend the corner to the backyard. The dots suddenly connect, and I don't give a shit that I have no shoes on and that, as soon as I step onto the lawn, dampness seeps in between my toes just like that of my dream. "You can't possibly think Killian has anything to do with kidnapping a woman? Or even the woman I hit?" I demand as soon as we step up to the B&B front door.

"Unlock it," Pierce says in a nice tone. I square my shoulders and narrow my eyes at him, ready to tell him where he can shove his warrant. There's no way Killian did this. Where would he even hide Susan?

He pinches the bridge of his nose. "Don't make this difficult, Tori. I-"

The B&B door opens, and Killian stands there, curiosity pinching his brows until he takes in Pierce with a sort of recognition. "Can I help you?" he rumbles to him in an irritated tone.

"They think you kidnapped a woman," I spit out.

Killian's eyebrows raise, and he directs his attention to Pierce, who tells him they have a search warrant to look around and through his things. Briefly, Killian closes his eyes, and then he opens the door wide for them to enter. The cops immediately dip inside and start digging through the space, and I come to stand beside Killian.

"He doesn't even have a car, you guys," I say to them. "You're looking for the wrong guy." It's on the tip of my tongue to have Pierce talk to his grandfather, but I know that will get me nowhere.

"Let them look," Killian grumbles. "They'll find nothing because there is nothing."

"I'm so sorry, Killian," I whisper as they dump his backpack contents onto the bed. "I can't believe – I – I'm so sorry."

He glances down at me consideringly. "Did you call them?"

I shake my head with wide eyes.

His expression softens. "Then you have nothing to be sorry for."

"I know, but I can't help but feel like this is my fault."

His head cocks to the side. "Why?"

I look down at my wet, bare feet. I could lie, but I have this sudden urge to confess. "Because I drew attention to you by asking Pierce to look into you when you first came into town."

For a moment, he stands there staring at the side of my face. My cheeks heat, but my gaze snaps up to his when he says, "I would have done the same thing."

"What?"

He shrugs. "You're a single woman, and a strange man asked to sleep behind you. You were protecting yourself."

Even though he's not trying to, what he says makes me feel

incredibly guilty. I pinch my lips between my teeth. "I asked him to stop, you know. I had changed my mind." He raises an eyebrow at me. "To stop looking into you, I mean. I figured you had your reasons for being so vague and that it was none of my business."

He nods again and turns his attention back to the cops. Stuff is strewn all over the space, and we watch in silence until they're done. Unsatisfied looks cover their faces when they make their way back to us, and we allow the other officers to pass through the door.

Pierce stops before us though and scratches the back of his neck. "Did you find anything?" I ask snootily when he makes no move to explain himself.

"I had to know for sure."

I place my hands on my hips. "And why the hell did you think it was him in the first place?"

He drops his hand back to his side and turns his attention to Killian. "Logically -"

"Oh, don't give me that 'logical' crap," I hiss. "You're a cop, Pierce. I'm not one, and I know exactly who you should be looking at and would refuse to."

A confused expression pinches Pierce's features before they smooth with understanding. "My grandfather didn't kidnap anyone, Tori. He doesn't even own a black van."

I shrug dramatically. "Neither does Killian, yet you thought he did."

He narrows his eyes at Killian, who has remained silent during our exchange. "Black vans are easy to hide when you live in the middle of nowhere. How did you get here, Killian?"

"By foot," he grumbles.

"And I'm supposed to believe that?"

I laugh without humor. "Until you find a black van with his prints all over it, you're going to have to. In the meantime, talk to your fucking grandfather."

He turns his narrowed eyes at me and considers me for a

moment as his anger brims under the surface. That's just fine with me because I'm sure it matches my own. "Can I talk to you for a minute?"

"Do I have to?"

He flicks his gaze toward Killian then back at me. "Yes."

"Fine," I mutter pissily. I stride out of the B&B and toward the back of my house. My feet are immediately covered in mud, but I'm so mad right now that I honestly don't care.

Pierce follows me, and once we are alone, Killian leaning against the doorframe watching us with his arms crossed, I abruptly ask Pierce, "What? What do you want?"

He widens his stance. "I think your judgment is off."

I slap my hands on my hips. "On what, Pierce?"

He glances behind him at Killian. "On him."

"Jesus fucking Christ," I mutter. "As far as you should be concerned, he's only a drifter. A tourist if you want to get fancy."

He turns back to face me with a scowl. "Why are you defending him?"

I match his expression. "Because you're dead wrong about him."

"I don't think so, Tori," he says, giving a shake of his head.

"You're wrong."

He considers me again, absorbing my stubborn tone, before he adds, "Do you have feelings for him?"

"What?" I practically yell, but even to my own ears, the half-denial sounds like a lie. I clear my throat and say again, "What the hell are you talking about?"

His shoulders lift and fall lazily, but I can tell this part of the conversation means more to him than Killian being a suspect. "It's a little obvious."

"It's none of your damn business, but do you know what is your business? There seems to be a hell of a lot of crime in this damn town, and you don't seem to be any closer to finding out the truth."

Even in the darkness, I can see his face redden as his anger rises. "If you knew what I knew about him, you'd-"

"I don't give a rat's ass what you found out about him." Because chances are it's colored with jealousy, the same jealousy that caused him to ask if I had feelings for Killian. "You seem to forget that this entire place is full of people. Killian isn't the only tourist; he just happens to be staying in town and not in the woods like everyone else." He looks down and flexes his jaw, so I add, "Look into them. Hell, look into the donut shop's owner if you have to. Do your job, and get the hell off my property."

He glances up from under his lashes and sees that he's no longer welcome. Giving a quick nod, he turns on his heel and strides away, but he stops next to Killian and murmurs, "This isn't over, Savage."

Chapter 16

Killian Savage

EVERY WORD of that sentence rubbed me the wrong way, and by the look on Tori's face, she had heard it. This guy knows nothing about me, yet he has it out for me. I didn't hear what he and Tori were talking about because their voices were too low, but I do know that whatever was said didn't make Tori particularly happy.

Growling under my breath, because not only did he piss off Tori, but he pissed off me, I stride after him. I don't give a shit if he has the law behind him. We have a few things to set straight.

He's almost to his car when I catch up to him. The other cops are already driving away, so the noise of their cars masked the sound of my feet on the gravel driveway.

The hinges squeal when Pierce opens the car's door, and he turns to face me with raised eyebrows. With the door between us, he leans his forearms against the rim of the top and waits for me to come to a full stop on the opposite side.

"What do you mean this isn't over?" I ask deeply, using the

question as more of a threat. I don't like it when people put their noses in my business, and that seems to be exactly what he's doing. He can fuck right off with that shit. I've done nothing to deserve it.

"It means that I don't believe you aren't involved in this somehow. Not for one second." His tone is calm and even because he knows that I can't do shit to him, no matter what he says. That doesn't mean I'm not fantasizing about it while I grind my teeth together.

"You found nothing," I remind him. "I don't even own a car."

He cocks his head to the side, and it matches his cocky attitude. "And why is that?"

I narrow my gaze to slits. "Because I don't need one."

The roll of his eyes only serves to irritate me more. "You know what I think, Savage? I think you don't own a car so that you can't be tracked."

With a flare of my nostrils, I continue to stare at him. I don't deny it, however, because it is a logical assumption. And the right assumption.

He continues, "I think that you don't want to be found by the people you worked for, and I think you don't want whoever or whatever it is you're chasing to know that you're coming."

"It's none of your concern."

"It is if you're kidnapping people to get what you want. You had to have picked up a few things from those who employed you. I can think of three people you worked for with that M.O. The question is: Are you doing it for someone, or is this a personal mission?"

My jaw flexes as he continues to contemplate. I won't give him shit, even though he's guessing correctly.

His face relaxes. "I think it's personal. I think you're on a mission to destroy whoever took your family from you."

"Don't act like you know everything," I growl dangerously.

He only shrugs. "Their obituaries weren't hard to find. Neither was the police report."

"Stay out of my business."

"Or what, Savage? You brought your business here as soon as you arrived, and shit started to get crazy. It's not a coincidence, and I'll prove exactly that."

I take a step toward him, hands balled into fists at my side. I never lose my cool. Never. But when the people I loved are brought up . . . "I don't care what you believe about me, but leave my family out of your mouth and out of your assumptions."

He flicks his gaze at Tori, who is still in the shadows of her house. "Does she know about them? About how they died and why? Does she even know they existed?"

"No," I answer honestly. "And you're not going to tell her."

He chuckles. "And why wouldn't I do that?"

I lift an eyebrow. "You know the people I worked for; you assume that I was involved in dirty work." I leave the threat open. Open enough that he grips the rim of the car tightly.

"Why do you care what she thinks of you?" I remain silent, and I can tell when it dawns on him. "You care about her."

"That's none of your business."

"It is if you break her heart."

I smirk a little, knowing I now have the upper hand because, by his tone, he doesn't like that I've grown close to Tori. That I might share something with her that he doesn't. I know a smitten fool when I see one. "I mean nothing to Tori."

"You're an idiot if you truly believe that." He leans into his forearms, and the door widens from his weight as he does. His eyes zoom in on the bracelet around my wrist. "She's fragile right now, and the last thing she needs is a drifter with a dead family and a past he's running from, trying to destroy her."

I have the urge to look back at her but refrain from doing so. His words struck something in me, something that would have caused me fear as soon as I stepped into this town. I hadn't meant for someone to gain feelings for me, and truth be told, I hadn't expected to gain anything for her either. Not enough so that I actually care if I'd hurt her by leaving like I plan to eventually.

Everything here has brought me nothing but trouble, so the logical choice would be to not stick around for much longer. I hadn't found what I needed here, except . . . Maybe I might have found something in Tori, and that's the reason why the very idea of leaving doesn't settle well with me. A friendship maybe, but anything more as he's implying? I don't think I'm capable of that anymore.

I hide my inner turmoil well by wiggling my fingers to remind myself that now isn't the time to think about this.

"Didn't even consider that, did you?" he grumbles. He leans back and makes to move into the driver's seat. "Watch yourself, Savage, or the town won't be the only thing you'll leave in ruins."

And with the last words, because I'm too speechless and lost in thought to rebut, he climbs into his car, starts it, and pulls out of the driveway. Once he's gone, I turn back around to look for Tori, but she's already gone.

With a quick glance, I see the kitchen light on in her house, and I sigh out a pent-up breath before I make my way back to the B&B.

Chapter 17

Tori Townsend

WITH ONE HAND, I slide the plate into my palm from the counter, and with the other, I grab the mug of steaming coffee. I know making him eggs and toast isn't the best apology, but there haven't been many things in my life that I've had to apologize for. I have no idea what I'm doing when it comes to any 'I'm sorry' gestures.

I could barely sleep last night. Hell, I was so embarrassed by the whole thing that I walked inside instead of waiting to see how the Pierce and Killian conversation ended. I couldn't hear what they were saying anyway, but I could tell that it wasn't a pleasant conversation. It was a conversation that likely had to do with me – by the way Pierce had been flicking his gaze in my direction. That was embarrassing too, knowing I was the topic of choice. I seem to be everyone's topic of choice lately.

I don't know how I manage it, but I somehow get the door open and uneasily make my way to the B&B front door. Once there, I bite my bottom lip and try to figure out how I'm going to knock on it when my hands are full. It makes me feel like an idiot, but I use my foot to knock, and it sounds more like I'm trying to break in than asking for access to the person inside.

It doesn't take long for the door to open, and standing there in nothing but his briefs is Killian. I can't help the way my eyes rake his body, tracing the hills and plains and the way the tattoos wrap around them. The nipple piercings glisten in the morning sun, and the scabs from our sex look to be healing nicely. The piercings aren't the only things that glisten. He's covered in a fine sheen of sweat, and by the way his veins are pronounced, he'd been working out.

And then there's the bulge between his legs… That bulge that twitches under the weight of my stare.

I gulp and slowly raise my gaze to his. "Hi," I squeak because who the hell could talk normally when he looks so damn edible? He isn't a fucking snack. He's a four-course meal.

"Hey," he rumbles. He places his hand on the door frame and leans a little weight into it. His corded muscles ripple, and it takes everything in me not to watch them shift.

Somehow, and don't ask me how because I have no idea, I manage to get my wits about me and raise the plate and the mug. "I have breakfast."

His eyebrows lift into his forehead. "For me?"

I nod, and he grins a small smile. "To apologize for last night."

Under his smile, he considers me for a moment before stepping aside. I nibble my bottom lip, wondering if I should even go inside or just pass him the plate. He waits as I make my decision, probably wondering what's going through my head that might explain why I haven't entered yet, but eventually, I give in. Even though I know it's a bad idea, I step inside his rented space.

The bed isn't made, so I imagine he hasn't been up long. A couple of pieces of clothing are lying on the floor like he stripped out of them last night after the shitshow that happened as he walked to the bed.

I twist my lips at the sight of them and say, "You know, I do have a washer and dryer you could use."

"I don't want to bother you, so I've been buying from Derek's store."

I turn to face him as I set the plate and mug on the table. "I have a perfectly good washer and dryer that you can use. You don't have to keep spending money, especially since I know that backpack of yours won't carry much more than what's stuffed in there."

My gaze drifts to the backpack that's brimming to its limit. I get the feeling it's always packed, so I don't mention anything about that. Instead, I say, "I really am sorry about last night. You have to know that I don't think you'd ever do such a thing."

From the corner of my eye, I see him shrug, so I drift my attention back to him. The way he's looking at me, the heat in his eyes as they rake over my body, makes me squirm a little. Warmth pools in my lower abdomen when he takes a step in my direction, and then another, a predator confidently stalking a prey that's too captivated to even move. "I really am sorry," I mutter again as he stands before me.

"Stop saying that," he huskily demands.

"I'm only saying it because I mean it," I murmur back. My mind goes to places… places that make my panties immediately wet. I squeeze my thighs together and hope like hell that I won't have a wet patch on my white shorts.

"You know what I think?" he asks, wrapping a hand around the back of my neck and tugging the roots of my hair at the nape. I all but moan, and my eyelids flutter as the sting of pain shoots right to my clit.

I shake my head.

"I think you came here to apologize, but you're staying because you can't stop imagining what a second time with me would be like. What it'd feel like. What core memory it'd make." He leans to whisper in my ear. "How I'd fucking destroy you and then ask you to go about your day with my cum drying between your legs."

Oh god. I shiver, and it only serves to prove him right. He chuckles and nips at my jaw. This time, the sting zaps straight to my nipples, and they pebble through my thin bra.

"Have you eaten?" he asks against my skin.

I shake my head again because there's no point in lying to him. I do, however, fail to admit that I've decided to try intermittent fasting. It was a decision I made last night while I lay in bed, unable to sleep after the night's events.

A low growl rumbles up his chest like he knows that I'm trying something new to lose weight. He barely knows me, yet he knows me.

Stepping away, he orders, "Take off your shorts and get on the table."

"What?"

A ghost of a smile tugs at the edges of his lips. "You're going to eat, and so am I."

I glance at the plate full of the food that I made solely for him. "But-"

He takes my chin and steers my attention back to him. "Take off your shorts, Tori, or I'll find a knife and cut them from you." He gives a small shake of his head, and for a second, his eyes downcast and skate over my body. When they return to mine, he adds, "And I won't be gentle."

Goosebumps rise over my skin, and just for a moment, I consider defying him just so I can experience that moment and have it live rent-free in my head. But then I find myself pushing my shorts and underwear down.

I kick them aside as he heads to the table and takes a seat in front of the plate. He scoots the plate to his left and pats the spot on the table where the plate was sitting only a second ago. "Sit," he orders.

Nervous butterflies flutter in my stomach, but again, I do what he asks. I cross the distance, slide between him and the table, and sit. Surprisingly, the table holds my weight.

"Now what?" I ask, my voice shaking with anticipation.

He wraps his palms against the top of my ass and scoots me to the edge. The slickness of my pussy slides against the table until he's satisfied with my position. And then he grips my knees and slowly spreads open my thighs. He takes in my dripping pussy with a hungry gaze. Heat pools and settles in my lower abdomen because that damn look . . .

With a lick of his lips like a starving man, he says, "Eat."

In the next second, he bends forward and nips my inner thighs, right at the juncture of my pussy. My thighs quiver for a moment, and I have the sudden urge to grip the back of his head and guide him to where I want him so desperately. It's hard, but I exercise patience.

Lazily, and as if he's taking his first lick of an ice cream cone, he skims my pussy with the edge of his tongue. When he reaches my clit, he nips it. I suck in a sharp breath, but it's cut short as his mouth latches onto the tight, throbbing bud that's begged for attention since the moment he opened my thighs. I inhale sharply at the sudden sensation and then moan when his tongue flicks against it, taking away the sting of his nip.

I lean back, balancing on the heel of my palms, and tip my head toward the ceiling as he sucks and flicks to the same song as my rapid-beating heart. Shuddering breaths escape me as he tugs on the most sensitive spot on my body with his mouth.

It's a reflex when I attempt to close my thighs around his head, making sure he doesn't move a damn inch, but he grasps my knees again and forces them apart, forcing me to take everything he's delivering.

My toes curl and uncurl, and my mouth falls open with a loud, tortured moan.

And then he stops.

My head whips up to look at him, an immediate protest on my tongue. His mouth and chin are coated in my arousal, and he must know that I'm about to beg him to keep going because he tips his eyes toward the forgotten plate by my hip. "Eat, or you won't get to cum."

I snap my mouth shut and glare at him. To test me or to tease me more, I'm not sure which one, he shoves a finger inside me and crooks it to massage that secret little spot. My eyes nearly roll into the back of my head, but his voice keeps me from completely falling apart. "Eat, Tori."

The slickness of my inner walls is telling him just how much I want this as he moves his fingers around inside me. Shakily, I pick up the fork and dip it into the eggs. Once I bring it to my mouth, he smirks like a cat who's got the cream and moves between my legs again.

He doesn't remove his fingers while the flat of his tongue slowly slides along my clit. I moan as I chew, and the sound is cut off when I swallow.

"Again," he orders against my soft flesh, his lips tickling.

I do exactly what he asks because I'll be damned if he stops. As a reward, he inserts another finger, and that delicious stretch and pressure makes my legs squeeze around him again.

His fingernails dig slightly into my knees, and his eyes lock with mine as he rumbles, "You'll eat, and you'll take every ounce I give you, Tori. Understood?"

Swallowing my bite, I nod and loosen my thighs once more. He dives between them and latches back on, and even though I barely register that I'm doing it, I eat.

Heat builds so heavily in my lower abdomen that my stomach tightens. I moan and groan around mouthfuls while I watch him feast on me. That sight alone makes my blood boil with pure, undiluted pleasure.

Every inch of my legs quivers and clench, and I beg him over and over again to not stop, to keep going. And when I explode against his face, the fork clatters against the plate, all but forgotten.

My abrupt scream as I orgasm makes my throat raw. My pussy walls tighten around his moving and crooked fingers, and my clit pulses against his tongue as he pulls every ounce out of me. I cum for what feels like forever, but he's patient and greedy and rides out the entire thing with me. And when I slump backward against the heels of my palms, his tongue slides down and licks up the mess I just created at my entrance.

Sliding his fingers out, he brings them to his mouth and licks them clean as he stands. I watch with hooded, sated eyes while he pushes down his briefs and frees his rock-hard length. He grabs my hips, lines himself up, and pushes inside with one smooth motion.

"Oh my god," I moan out because that stretch and pressure of his cock is even more delicious than his fingers.

"Fuck," he hisses. His fingers are bruising my hips as he holds onto what appears to be sanity. "You're still pulsing."

Together, we watch as he pulls out, glistening, and pushes back in. His entire length is swallowed by my pussy, and aside from feeling it, just witnessing it is better than anything I've drummed up when I take care of myself.

The table groans as he picks up the pace until he's slamming into me. Knowing exactly what he likes, I take the fork and drag the pointed edges down his chest to just above the scabs from the other night. His eyelids flutter as welts rise across his skin, and he whispers his pleasure in words that I can't understand.

I do it again and again while he pounds into me, leaving trails of red that are almost masked by the tattoos. Muscles ripple and shift as I take him in. This powerful man, this man with so many secrets, could break me in more ways than one. Instead of being scared of it like any normal person, I embrace it. At least, for this moment, while he is slamming into me and his cock rubs just the right spot.

My lower abdomen coils, and my breath picks up pace. Aside from the sound of our bodies joining together, all I can hear is my blood rushing through my ears. I can't take my eyes off my pussy swallowing his cock. I can't think of anything else but the way this feels.

I'm so close, so damn close, and I'm just about to raise my gaze and tell him that when he reaches between us and presses a thumb to my clit. It's enough to send me crashing into my orgasm. The fork clatters to the ground, and I grab his forearms as I scream once again.

I barely hear his deep groan while my pussy ripples and milks his cock. He moves faster, slamming into me so hard that the table moves with us. He lifts his gaze away from our union and locks them with mine. His lips part, and his eyebrows pull together, and then he's pulling out. I watch with interest as he pumps himself the rest of the way. His cum spurts out and hits me on the top of my pussy and all over my inner thighs, and I freaking live for it.

When he's finished, he smears his cum all over my inner thighs like frosting then puts his wet fingers to my lips. "Eat," he orders with so much heat in those damn words that I open my mouth and suck his cum off his fingers. Salt explodes on my tongue, and I swallow, refusing to take my eyes off his. While I clean his fingers, he hums in approval.

Eventually, he pulls them out and replaces them with his lips, giving me one, lingering kiss.

And my heart fucking melts.

Chapter 18

Killian Savage

I DRESS WHILE SHE DOES. I kissed her after sex, and this time it was different than the other times our lips met. I can't put my finger on it – why it was different – but I know that it meant something to her too. I saw it in her eyes when I pulled away. It makes me wonder what my own face looked like if I looked as confused as I felt because I haven't felt this way since the last time I kissed my wife. That was the morning of the day she died. The day that changed everything.

Kissing her feels like being pulled from a coffin I buried myself alive in. Because I deserved it. Because I belonged there. But the moment she's in my space, I feel relief. Fresh oxygen. The fading of fear. The pull back from the slow suicide I've been striving for when I put myself in that coffin in the first place.

I didn't know I was walking a dark path until her. It doesn't turn my mind from the man I'm trying to find, and it doesn't change my outlook on life, but it does make me feel like I found a home when I didn't feel like that'd ever be possible again. A home *in her.*

How am I supposed to leave her now? It may just be the hardest thing I'll ever do, and I've done a lot of difficult things, but I promised myself I'd make that man pay. While standing on their fresh graves, I swore to my dead wife and kids that I'd make him suffer.

I push back a few loose strands of hair and turn to face her as she buttons up her shorts. When she's finished, she swivels on her heels to me with her lips twisted to the side.

"What?" I ask, a little amused by the expression.

"I swear to god that I never do this."

I cock my head to the side. "Do what?"

She cringes. "I never sleep with a guy twice." The grin I wear makes her laugh. "What?"

"Does that mean you like me?" I tease.

Her face sobers, and I know then that what she's going to say next does not play along with my joke. She's serious when she admits in a murmur, "I shouldn't. I don't even know you, and . . ."

"And what?" I murmur back. It's the only volume I can muster because, for some odd reason, my heart patterns a different beat, waiting on bated breath as she bares the truth.

Her shrug is small. "You won't even share anything with me about yourself. I know nothing about you."

I consider her carefully. "But you like me anyway?"

She crosses her arms and looks down at her feet as she toes the floor. "I shouldn't. By all rights, I shouldn't be more than attracted to you."

"You're right," I whisper. "You shouldn't."

She raises her gaze to mine and studies me for a second. "Why?"

I clench my jaw because denying her what she's feeling isn't an easy thing to do. "I'm not the marrying type. I'm not the happily-ever-after guy. Not anymore."

Her brows pinch together. "What do you mean?" I say nothing. I don't want to burden her with my past, especially with Pierce's words echoing in my head as a warning about how fragile she is. Because he's not wrong. "What happened? What can't you tell me?"

"You don't need to know that."

Angrily, she looks away. I'm relieved to have her attention off of me, but that relief quickly fades when her gaze lands on the picture that's resting on the nightstand. She travels to it, unfolds her arms, and gingerly picks it up.

I freeze as she studies the picture of my family. Eventually, she turns to me. "Are these – Are you – Is this your wife? Your family?" The accusatory tone settles in the pit of my gut like a rock.

"Yes."

"You're married?" she hisses.

I rake a hand through my tied-up hair, messing it up more than sex and working out had. "Was."

The frown returns to her face, and she opens her mouth to say something but snaps it shut and returns to studying the picture. After a pause, she asks, "You got divorced? Wait . . ." She lifts her eyes back to mine. "I don't understand. If these are your kids, why are you so far from them?"

My hand slides down to my face and swipes at my now-stressed expression that pulls my cheeks taut. "They don't need me anymore."

"Why? I don't understand, Killian."

I drop my hand back to my side. "Because I buried them before I left."

I watch as her throat constricts in a heavy swallow. "And your wife?"

"Her too," I mutter.

"Oh, Killian." I barely hear her voice, but more clearly, she adds, "I didn't know. I-I'm so sorry."

My shrug is my only answer because how do I explain to

her everything that happened? How it was my fault? How I wasn't there when they needed me?

She gently sets the picture back down. "How'd they die?"

"They were murdered," I manage to say.

She doesn't look at me for a second, but when she does, her expression is full of sorrow. "How?"

I sigh and head to the bed. The mattress dips when I take a seat and balance my elbows on my knees. "What I did for a living had consequences that I never thought about. I thought I was careful. Even Larissa had no idea what I was doing because I was protecting her. Protecting *them*. In the end, it got them killed."

She comes to sit on the edge of the bed with me. Her tone sounds almost like she's not sure if she wants to know, but she asks anyway, "What did you do for a living, Killian?"

I open my palms and stare at the lines across them. "I was a private interrogator. Hired mainly by New York's worst."

"Oh," she breathes. I'm sure her mind is going through all the scenarios of what the job implies. I give her credit; she doesn't scoot away. "The pain thing. It's why you like it. You're punishing yourself for everything you'd done to others."

I shrug a little because, honestly, I'd never thought about it. The way my brain works has never been something I'd dwelled on too long because I don't like what I find when I do.

"How did it kill your family?" she asks when I don't verbally admit anything.

I clench and unclench my fingers, letting my nails bite into my palms as the memories resurface and the way their bodies were lying for me when I arrived home to find them dead. Each was holding a lily petal in their palm as blood spread out around them from their stab wounds.

I breathe out slowly. "I interrogated a man who had kidnapped a crime lord's niece. He never admitted to anything, but I had enough information on him to know that he impregnated the women he stole off the streets. Kept the children as his own." I chuff. "The sickest part was he used to be a gynecologist." I look at her. "Rumor has it that his first kidnapping was one of his patients."

She gulps. "And then what?"

"Somehow, he figured out who I was. Where I lived. I don't know how he did it, I don't know how he learned it, but I came home to a dead wife and two dead sons."

"Jesus," she breathes. "How do you know it was him?"

"There were signs," I say because she doesn't need the dirty details etched into her mind. The last thing I need is for her to fear me more than she already might.

"Does their death have anything to do with you traveling the States?" I know she's just trying to understand me since I'm giving her the information so freely, but the probing is painful.

I'm sure my expression is hard when I turn my head to look her in the eye. What I find is nothing but concern. "Something like that."

She nods again, knowing that's the best answer I can give. She doesn't need to know that I plan to put my skills to use one last time. Make him suffer. Make him pay. The begging for his life will be far better than the gush of his last dying breath.

"Thank you," she eventually says.

I hadn't expected that, so I scowl at her. "For what?"

"For being honest. I hadn't come here for that, but I need you to know one thing."

"And what's that?"

She leans forward and presses a soft kiss to my cheek. "I'm not the marrying type either." When she pulls away, she adds, "I would never expect you to change for me, to tarnish the memory of your wife by taking another, for however long this lasts before you leave to do . . . whatever it is you're doing. I know this is temporary – I know that – but I want to give in to what I'm feeling because it just feels right. I just want to do something that feels right while everything else around me is so wrong."

"Okay," I rumble because I can understand that. I'd be lying if I said that I didn't want the same thing. It'll make it harder to leave, but moments with her to remember and look back on will be worth it.

She smiles a little. "Okay." Gripping my knee, she stands up. "I have to go meet Derek, but I'll see you later?"

I nod, and it's almost on the tip of my tongue to ask her to stay, but I don't. I know she has a lot to think about, a lot to sift through concerning everything I just told her, so I remain silent as she makes her way to the door.

With one last glance at me, she heads out, and I'm left there with nothing but memories, a picture, and a backpack full of everything I have left.

Chapter 19

Tori Townsend

AS I WALK into my little store, I contemplate all things that are Killian Savage. He wasn't wrong about yesterday. After meeting with Derek, I had gone to work with cum making my thighs stick together, but after that? When I got home? I hadn't seen him, and I'd been so exhausted from the night before that I fell asleep before the notification came of my cameras picking him up on his return to the B&B.

I sigh deeply when I breathe in the shop's familiar and comforting smells. I hadn't seen him this morning either. Minus the camera. I neither confirm nor deny that I may have watched him leave. I may have been making a small breakfast as I caught up on paperwork for both businesses when my camera dinged his departure. I have no idea where he goes during the day, but I don't blame him for wanting to leave the little house that he's bunking in. There isn't a TV or radio. It's designed for tourists who never stay long between those four walls. Who goes on vacation and stays only in the place they're renting? No one, and certainly not Killian.

Maybe he goes for a hike? Maybe he just walks around? Either way, I try not to make it my business even though that's hard.

Instead, I paste on a smile as Tegan looks up from behind the counter and grins at my arrival. It's early evening, and her and Josiah's shift is over. I'll be closing up the shop today, a rare night shift. I love this shop, I truly do, but I don't like having my nights taken from me. But really? What else am I going to do? I'll just be working from home. I might as well have a desk to sit at while I do it.

"Hey," I greet, and the sound of my voice makes Josiah's head pop around a triangle display case.

His eyes basically sparkle when they land on mine, and just to appease his puppy-dog love, I pat him on the shoulder as I pass by.

"You're earlier than I expected," Tegan responds, turning her gaze toward her wristwatch.

"I got a little bored at home." I head toward the back of the shop and open my office door. Tegan follows close behind as I flick on the lights, illuminating my messy space. I stand there for a moment, taking in the disaster across my desk, and slump my shoulders as I make my way to it.

"What's wrong with you?" she whispers. "You seem super down."

"It's just this mess. I should do something about it tonight."

I drop my purse on top of a pile of crap and stare down at the hours of work I have ahead of me strewn across the surface of my desk.

She approaches. "I feel like it's more than that."

Twisting my lips from side to side, I contemplate whether I'm even going to respond to that. Choosing to because I don't keep anything from Tegan, I look up and meet her stare. "My life is just as much of a mess."

A sympathetic look relaxes the lines across her forehead. "I know. You have a lot going on with, you know . . . that woman and then your two businesses."

I wave a hand in the air as if I'm batting at an invisible fly and then shrug.

She scowls. "Is there more?"

I nibble the inside of my cheek. I could easily deny it, but sometimes Tegan has great advice, and I could really use some. "Killian."

Her scowl deepens. "What about him?"

My cheeks heat, and I swear to shit that, if color is rising in them, I'll disown my own body. "I slept with him again."

The scowl is wiped from her face, and she blinks at me owlishly. "You never do that," she breathes. "One guy? Twice? What . . . Oh my god, you – you like him."

I look down at my desk because the truth behind her words, the realization in her eyes, gives me butterflies in the pit of my gut. I haven't decided if I like those butterflies yet.

I open my mouth for the usual denial, but her finger pointing at me cuts me off. "Don't even try it. You never sleep with a guy twice, Tori. I believe your very words were, 'It makes things messy.'"

"That's because it does," I grumble. I grab my fingers and twist them around, suddenly taken over with a nervous energy because my current life is just evidence that it does.

She crosses her arms over her chest and shifts her weight so her hip pops in a sassy way. Her shirt is a little tighter today, and I can see a slight baby bump poking out from underneath. "I don't get what the problem is."

I narrow my eyes at her. "I don't want what I'm doing to mean anything."

Her smile is small. "But you and I both know that it does."

"How do I stop it?" I groan out with a sag of my shoulders.

"Why do you want to stop it?"

I pinch the bridge of my nose as I try to figure out how to

word it so that she understands. "I don't trust men. They've always let me down. First, my step-father and the way he treated me as if I wasn't his daughter and I was a house pet. Then my asshole ex." I drop my hand back to my side. "I can feel myself getting clingy toward Killian. Greedy even. And I know in the end that it'll only leave me more scarred than I already am."

"And why is that?"

"Because he's going to leave." I throw my hands in the air and slap them at my sides, a display of how obvious my statement was.

"Well, if it helps, Cole doesn't like him."

I chuckle without any humor. "Not helpful at all. Cole doesn't like anyone."

She considers me carefully. "Why do you think so far into the future? Why can't you just enjoy something that is in the now?"

"I'm in the business of business. I've trained myself to look into the future. That's not a habit I can just break."

"You know what I think?" she asks, and I shake my head as I stride past her to walk back out into the shop. Josiah is still here. He doesn't look our way as he finishes up dusting. "I think your accident and that woman's life ending put a different perspective on life for you. Like, how no one claimed that woman and how you're drawing a parallel that that could possibly happen to you."

I step behind the counter and turn to face her. "Maybe," I say while nibbling on the corner of my lips.

She grabs a stray hair that's resting against my cheek and tucks it behind my ear. "I think that scares you, and you're clinging to someone that you could feel like they'd protect you. It's perfectly natural."

I shrug. "And I just really like him. He's different. Puzzling." I run a hand across my cheek. "I don't even know what I'm talking about."

She grins. "It's okay to like him."

"Yeah," I sigh out. I give myself a little shake. "Let's talk about something else. Did the mail come?"

"Yeah," Josiah says from across the store. I hadn't been aware that he'd been listening, but Tegan and I turn to face him anyway. "It's under the register."

"Thanks," I say, and he goes back to dusting as if he hadn't been eavesdropping at all.

I grab the mail and start leafing through it when the shop's door opens and lets in a cold, rainy breeze. "Speak of the devil," Tegan whispers next to me.

"Huh?" I ask, tipping my head up from the mail to look at her. She's staring at the door, so I turn to look with her. Killian stands there, taking in the store and the trinkets and books it offers. "Shit," I add under my breath.

Once his eyes land on me, he strides in my direction.

I hear Tegan giggle quietly before she blurts, "I'm going to go now."

"Asshole," I mutter back to her.

All she does is wink, grab her purse from under the counter, and slide past Killian on her way out. He watches her go, and I look around nervously, spotting Josiah moving closer to where Killian and I now stand, the counter separating us.

Raindrops cover his leather jacket and dampen his hair, but it only makes him look sexier. It also only makes me want him more. "What are you doing here?" I ask after I get my wits about me. I hadn't expected to see him so soon, not after the conversation Tegan and I just had, and certainly not at my shop. "How did you even get here?"

He turns his attention back to me. "I walked."

I frown. "Really?"

A small grin plays at the edge of his lips. "No. I was at Derek's store, and he offered me a ride. Something about going to the hardware store."

"Right," I say.

"Did you get that part for the car?"

I suck in a quick breath and press a hand to my forehead. "Oh my god, I had completely forgotten."

He shrugs a little. "I'll pick it up."

"You don't have to do that."

He shrugs again. "It's not a problem."

I sweep his expression and find nothing but sincerity, so I say, "Thank you. Is the car part the only reason you wanted to come here?"

His jaw flexes a little, but his eyes are soft. I can tell he doesn't want to admit it when he says, "No."

I tuck my lips between my teeth to hide my smile and the butterflies that are slamming against the lining of my stomach. Maybe I do like them after all. "No? Did you come to see me?"

"I came to see the shop." He gazes around for a moment again, briefly lingering on Josiah.

I chuff. "You came to see me. Admit it."

His eyes don't return to mine, but a smile does peek through his hidden expressions.

Josiah shifts a little, and my gaze moves to him for a split second. He's watching the interaction, listening to every word as his duster is poised to dust a shelf he's probably already gotten to. His eyes are a little wide, fearful if I had to guess, but then again, it's not every day you see a man like Killian striding through this area.

Killian picks up a trinket, drawing my attention back to him as he examines the sharp angles of the miniature statue. "Is Derek giving you a ride home? I mean, I can, but it'll be a couple of hours."

He places the statue back on the counter, and his gaze pierces mine. My heart skips a beat because I swear to god he can see within my soul. There's no way he doesn't see that I'm greedy for him – just like I confessed to Tegan.

"Sure," he answers.

"What are you going to do after you get the part?"

"Walk around town."

I chuckle a little. "Walking must be your favorite thing."

"Gives me time to think."

"That's a lot of thinking," I say with raised eyebrows.

He only raps his knuckles against the counter and starts backing his way toward the shop's door. "See you in a few hours."

I nod, almost too eagerly, and he smirks a little as he pushes open the door with his back and steps outside. I watch him through the windows as he heads down the sidewalk toward the hardware store and release a pent of breath before turning my attention to Josiah.

"I can do the rest of the dusting if you want to go?" I ask him.

His eyes are solely on the spot where Killian disappeared, so I snap my fingers to gain his focus. "You okay?" I ask as he turns to face me. His face is a little white.

"Yeah," he says, his voice cracking a little. He lowers the duster back to his side.

My frown pulls my eyebrows together. "Do you know Killian?" Because, by the way he's reacting, it's as if Killian killed his cat.

He shakes his head. "No, but I recognize his type."

I pinch my lips together, feeling a bit defensive for Killian. "Never judge someone you don't know, Josiah."

I watch as he swallows thickly, but he nods anyway. He heads to the counter and sets the duster down. I pluck his wallet from underneath and pass it to him. "Thanks for coming in today." My tone is a little grumpy, but I don't like how he talked about someone he doesn't even know. "Do you have an umbrella?"

He shakes his head as he slides his wallet into his back pocket. "I have a raincoat in my car though."

"Good. See you tomorrow?"

He nods as he heads toward the door, and the moment I'm alone, I place my elbows against the counter's surface and sag my weight into it. I almost wish walks worked for me, too. My head is so full, and I have absolutely no idea how to compartmentalize or process it.

Chapter 20

Killian Savage

FROM THE PASSENGER SEAT, I find myself looking over at Tori as she drives in the direction of her home back in Fairview. She's quiet, lost in her own thoughts, so I let her have them and remain quiet as she works through whatever she's feeling at the moment. If she felt like telling me, she would have by now.

Rain sprinkles on the windshield, and the only sound is the wipers swaying across the glass. I find myself watching it tickle the surface and not paying attention to where we're going until she pulls onto the side of the road. I scowl as I look outside the window and find the wet field of lilies to my right.

"What are we doing?" I ask, breaking the silence with a rumbling murmur.

She leans back in the seat, sighs, and looks up at the roof of the car. Then, she tips her head in my direction and gives me a small smile. "Want to sit on our bench with me?"

Our bench. I didn't miss that. It makes the hair on my arms stand on end, and it has nothing to do with ill feelings. Deep down, however, I know that we shouldn't share anything together. We shouldn't indulge in each other. But with her looking at me, waiting for my response, I can't deny her what she wants and, frankly, what I want too.

I give a curt nod, and her smile grows. She shuts off the car, and together, we climb out.

The sprinkles are cool on the back of my neck as we make our way to the field. As soon as we reach the bench, she giggles a little under her breath, takes my hand, and pulls me toward the flowers. Curious enough, I allow her to lead me into their depths. We squelch our way through until we near the middle, and then she whirls, gathers herself on her toes, and presses her lips to mine.

I'm so surprised by this mood that I freeze for a second. Between her quiet thoughtfulness and this sudden need for comfort… whatever she'd been thinking about she now needs to be distracted from. So, I give her what she wants because, again, I can't deny her anything it would seem, and kiss her back.

When she breaks the kiss, I ask, "What's going on?"

She shakes her head and lets go of my hand. "Nothing," she says as she crosses her legs, sits in the dirt, and messes up a patch of flowers. "Sit with me?"

I raise an eyebrow. "In the mud?"

She shrugs. "Live a little, Killian."

I grind my teeth just once, knowing I've lived more of a life than any normal person. But all my memories are things no one should have to endure, and this seems to be good-hearted and good-natured. I don't comment on any of this as I take a seat, however, because I don't need to bring her to the center of my own burdens.

The wet dirt immediately soaks my jeans while I place my legs on either side of her knees and yank her closer to me.

A mischievous grin surfaces on her face before she reaches

and pushes my jacket off my shoulders. The sleeves gather at my elbows, and I raise my eyebrows at her.

She doesn't answer my silent question when she whispers, "Take it off."

I do as she asks, letting her steer whatever this is – even though I have a feeling I know *exactly* what this is. I ball it up, set it beside me, and look at her expectedly.

"Shirt," she adds just as quietly.

I gather the bottom of my shirt in my palms and lift it over my head. The sprinkles immediately cool my heating skin, and my cock starts to harden at the direction this is going.

Her gaze sweeps over my torso, taking in the tattoos and the muscles shifting as I place my shirt on top of my jacket.

Without a word, she reaches out and runs her fingers over the scabs. "Does it hurt?"

"Only in a good way," I respond because it's the truth. Every time I feel the pull of skin against the scabs, I'm turned on. I remember our time together and dream about a second round of pain. And the fact that I know that she liked delivering my pain only heightens my current arousal.

Her gaze flicks to mine, and I can see the lust in their depths. She leans back a little and her fingers dip into her pocket. Carefully, she pulls out a small boxcutter. "Do you want some more?"

"Did we come here just for this?"

She lifts one shoulder and lets it fall lazily. "Unbutton your jeans."

Normally, I don't take direction when it comes to sex, but something in her voice tells me she needs this as much as I want this. Whatever the reason, I don't deny her. I lean back and unbutton my jeans then wait for further instructions.

"Push them down a little."

For a second, I *do* consider denying her because my ass will be covered in mud. But it's already wet from the dampness through the fabric, so there's really no point. I lift my ass and slide the jeans down, dragging my briefs with them. My cock springs free, and I grit my teeth against how good it feels to have the raindrops pepper my shaft.

I watch as her tongue darts out and wets her lips. Like she's hungry. Like she wants it more than air. I hide my smirk well because I want nothing more than to give it to her.

Leaning back on one elbow in the mud, I grab my shaft with my other hand and glide it up and down. Her lips part as she takes in my motions, an invitation to do whatever it is she has planned next.

"What are you going to do, dollface?" I rumble heatedly when she makes no move but to greedily watch me pleasure myself.

From the heaviness of her stare, from the cool drizzle, and from the slide of my hand, precum gathers at my tip. She leans forward and licks it up, and I cannot help the moan that comes out of my mouth.

Her finger flicks the boxcutter's lever, and the blade pushes out of the top. A shiver rakes down my entire body, making my cock twitch and my nipples strain against their piercings.

With the box cutter's tip, she trails the blade across my balls. I suck in a sharp breath, knowing she didn't cut the skin but loving the sharp sting anyway. My balls tighten, and my cock hardens more in my fist. I continue pumping, watching eagerly as she drags the blade to my inner thigh. Moving her gaze to my face, she slowly slices.

My eyelids flutter closed, and I breathe a sigh of relief as pain sears me. My hand pumps a little harder, and she makes another cut just beside it before moving to my other thigh. "Fuck," I groan out as she cuts into my skin. She makes another cut, and another, and I can feel the blood dripping down my legs and onto the mud below me.

The pain is everything. The pain is breath; it's freedom.

Gently, she sets the boxcutter to the side and gathers herself onto her knees. Mud coats her pants, but she doesn't seem to mind as she swirls her tongue around my tip. She nudges my hand away, so I lean back on both elbows and get the full view of what she's about to do to me.

She grabs my base and applies pressure, and then she slides her mouth down my length. "Fuck," I groan again as the warmth of her mouth, the wetness of her tongue, raises goosebumps all over my abdomen.

Her eyes move to mine, and she takes in how my lips part, how my eyes blink slowly so that I don't miss a beat of her mouth around me. And then she starts to move, her head bobbing as her hand around my base moves to my balls. She grabs hold of them, kneads them, and gently pulls. She's rewarded with a moan that I just can't help.

With her free hand, she moves it up my wet jeans until her fingertips skim the bloody cuts along my inner thigh. When she digs her nails into them, I buck against her mouth and tip my head back toward the sky. The pain travels all the way up to my navel and tightens my balls so tight that I'm surprised they're still outside of my body.

Her head bobs faster, and I raise a muddy hand and grip the hair at the back of her head, aiding her – no, demanding her – to make me cum. To tip me over the damn edge I'm riding thanks to her.

Her nails dig in further, and her teeth scrape against my shaft. I grit my teeth to keep all the sounds I want to make from spilling out of my mouth. She's never done this to me before, but somehow she knows exactly what I want.

Unable to help myself, I lean back a little farther on my elbow and shove her down my length as far as she can go. I hold her there, groaning as her throat constricts while she fights for air. Curses spill out of my mouth, despite my desperate attempt to keep them in.

When I allow her up, she doesn't complain. She doesn't back off my cock. She resumes with heavy breaths, and she works my cock with more determination than she had before.

A tingle begins at the base of my spine, and I murmur what a good job she's doing between short little pants. My grip on her hair tightens, and it has to be painful, but she says nothing. She doesn't even wince.

And when she takes me in further than I had shoved her and gags, I groan so deeply that my nipple piercings vibrate as I explode down her throat. She drinks every drop as I watch her, our eyes locked in the usual way as something passes between us that I don't fully understand.

Once I've finished, my cock pops out of her mouth, and she sits back on her ankles with a satisfied look. It takes a minute for words to form in my thoughts, but once they do, I say, "Satisfied, dollface?"

She nods eagerly and observes as I slide my jeans back up my muddy ass and fasten the button once more. "Are you?"

I raise an eyebrow. "Did it look like I didn't enjoy it?"

A small smile takes over her face, but she doesn't respond. Instead, she takes her bloody fingers and wipes them on lily petals. Immediately, their pristine white surface is coated in red, and she peers at the contrasting colors with interest.

"Tori," I murmur, drawing her attention back to me.

"Hmm?" she asks when our gazes meet.

"What's this about?" I ask because she's clearly going through something, and though I usually don't involve myself with other people's problems, she's different.

She looks away and bites her bottom lip. Instead of answering me, she looks back at me, her eyes on my wrist. They widen a fraction. "You're still wearing the bracelet?"

I lift my wrist. "Yeah."

She touches her face with her muddy hand. "I thought you would have taken it off by now."

"Why?" Honestly, I don't know why I'm still wearing it. Jewelry has never been my thing.

"You just don't seem the type to wear something that means protection."

"What type do I seem?"

She shrugs and glances at my chest. "With the cross tattoo on your sternum, I figured you were the godly type."

I consider my next words carefully because she could either take it the right way or the wrong way. "My wife was. I got it for her when she died."

"Why?"

It's my turn to shrug. "Because I have to believe that she went to heaven the way she thought she would."

She nods a little, and relief fills me that she didn't, in fact, take it the wrong way. I grab my now-wet shirt and slide it over my head. Next, I put on my muddy jacket. When I gather myself to my feet, I hold out my hand for her to take. She does, and I lift her, and together, we silently stride back for the car.

Once we're in the car, she breaks our momentary silence by starting the engine. "Thanks for replacing the car part while I worked," she says.

I murmur, "You're welcome." It hadn't taken me long, and the hardware store let me borrow the tools I needed. I'm surprised that a hardware store would even order a part for a car, but since there isn't an auto parts store in Mount Pleasant or Fairview, they probably get good business by doing so.

She pulls out onto the road and steers the car back toward Fairview. "My employee is scared of you," she comments, switching subjects so fast that I flick my gaze toward the side of her face.

"I'm a terrifying guy."

She shakes her head. "Not to me."

I look back out the windshield. "If you knew what I'd done to get answers for my job, you would be."

She's quiet for a moment, and I can feel that she wants to ask me, but she refrains from doing so. I'm not sure I'd tell her anyway. No one needs to know about it, especially not a woman I care for.

"Can I ask you something?" she eventually asks.

"Sure," I respond tentatively.

"Who killed your family?"

Discretely, I blow out a shaky breath, and a familiar pain pings in my chest. But instead of ignoring the question, I decide to be honest and answer. "The Lillian."

She looks over at me for a second before she returns her attention to the road. "Who's that?"

I shift in my seat uncomfortably. "He believes himself to be a pure man, but a man is not truly pure if they have to hide their true identity in my opinion. Out of everything I did to him, I never learned what his true name was because he had many false names, even going as far as using one for his practice. Without his true name, he's been hard to track down since he left the coast. Makes you wonder why he had the false names to begin with."

"That's what you're doing? Tracking him and not wandering aimlessly?"

I nod. "I will find him. He'll mess up."

"I believe you," she whispers. "Do you know anything about him?"

"I know he wasn't working alone. I could tell by his pale skin that he rarely left his house. At least, not during the day. But someone was doing the kidnapping, and I don't know if it was him or someone else. I'm sure he wasn't working alone though, but even the information I did get from him wasn't much. He could endure a lot of pain."

"What was the most important information?"

I twitch my lips, remembering the burn on the side of his face that I'd given him for it. "A lily. He'd leave them one and then later kidnap them. The sick fuck would even brand the women with the flower."

She's so quiet when my voice trails off, and I shift a little to study her face. It's pale, and her eyes are wide. The next second later, her foot hits the gas.

"Tori? What are you doing?"

"The brand."

"What about it?"

She peers at me for a second, her expression fearful. "The woman I hit had the same one. We have to tell Pierce."

Chapter 21

Tori Townsend

PIERCE LOOKS at us from the other side of his desk as he takes in everything I just blurted to him. Even though we're covered in mud, he hasn't commented on it.

It's dim in his office, the sun having set on our way here, and the rain is coming down harder than the earlier drizzle-mist. It pelts against the window, making my entire speech that much more daunting.

"I think you've spent too much time around those flowers, Tori," he murmurs while rising to his feet, popping his eyes back and forth between us and pointing at the mud across our faces with them.

"Excuse me?" I ask with a wide, disbelieving expression. I thought I'd get some resistance, but a complete dismissal wasn't on my list of ideas of what to expect.

"You've been spending a lot of time there." He waves a hand to soothe the sting of his words, but it does nothing of the sort. "The whole town talks about it."

"That is simply a coincidence, Pierce. The brand and the

field have nothing to do with each other."

He considers me again then turns a slightly narrowed gaze at Killian. Killian doesn't shift under the weight of his silent accusation. He simply stares back, unafraid that he has a badge. The handcuffs. The gun. "You saw this 'Lillian'?"

"Yes," Killian rumbles with a tinge of annoyance.

"Here?"

He shakes his head, though I can tell he wishes he could tell him otherwise.

Pierce puckers his lips for a moment, and it accentuates his five o'clock shadow. "Are you going to tell me how you've seen him and where?"

Kilian's face remains blank as he says, "No."

Pierce pinches the bridge of his nose, and I take the opportunity to intervene. "You have to believe us, Pierce."

Over his fingers, he studies me before dropping his hand back to his side. To Killian, he asks exasperatedly, "What do you know about him?"

"Not much," Killian answers after a moment. "Just that he barely left his house." He goes on to explain how he managed to catch him the first time, completely eludes the torture part and the reason behind it, but goes on to explain what the Lillian does to his hostages.

It turns out that when he caught him, he'd been trolling for another woman, 'hunting her,' he called it.

"He wasn't working alone," Killian finishes.

"What makes you say that?"

Killian glances at me, and for a second, I almost think he doesn't want to answer so that he doesn't scare me. He doesn't need to do that, though. I'm scared enough as it is. "He'd need someone to watch the women he keeps. He can't hunt and watch them at the same time."

Pierce twitches his nose as though he hadn't considered that. "Any idea of who it is?"

Killian goes to shake his head but, unable to help myself, I blurt through a humorless laugh, "Oh, I have my ideas."

Pierce switches his attention to me with a raised eyebrow. "And?"

I cross my arms over my chest. "Your grandfather."

He tips his head back and laughs. "And what would be your evidence of that?"

I shrug, a little offended by him finding this funny. "You two are the only new ones in town. I saw a tall man in a bright orange raincoat, and though everyone seems to have one, he fits that category." I glance at Killian, remembering our conversation in the car. "And you all are from the same area. He's a purist just like the Lillian."

He shakes his head slowly. "He doesn't own a black van, Tori."

I shrug again. "Like you said, it'd be easy to hide one."

Lifting a hand, he rubs the back of his neck as I throw his words back at him.

"How long ago did you live with your grandfather?" I press on. I take a step toward his desk and splay my hands across it as I lean in his direction. "You have no idea what he could be doing now."

A red hue colors his cheeks. "Don't you think I'd know if my grandfather was stealing women? Breeding them like cattle?" He sighs out his pent-up negative energy. "I get it. You don't like him, but all you have is a coat everyone has, a threat of being unclean because of your lifestyle, and the area we lived in before. If anything, you've got him for harassing you."

Killian growls in disbelief.

Pierce only flicks a moment of attention at him before returning to me. He jabs his finger in Killian's direction. "Besides, I'd bet my last dollar that the way he obtained any information on this guy wasn't legal. It's not enough for a warrant on my grandfather, and all the other evidence leads us to nowhere."

"But-"

He slices a hand through the air. "You've got nothing, Tori, and I've got nothing on the woman with the brand. I'm sorry, but you're dead wrong."

Chapter 22

Killian Savage

I PARK the car at her house and turn off the engine. I offered to drive from the police station, and she was so lost in thought that she didn't object. The whole way home, which was only a few minutes, she hasn't said a word, and I can't find a single reason to blame her.

While Pierce has a point, I have a gut feeling that he's wrong. However, I don't even know if the Lillian is here. He could have just been passing through when Tori hit one of his women, but I know one thing for certain: I am getting close.

I glance over at her, knowing that if I'm close, I'm that much closer to leaving this town and continuing my search, which means leaving her.

Rubbing at the ache in my chest, I climb out of the car and into the rain. Once I'm around to the other side, I open her door and offer her my hand. She takes it, and I don't know why I do it, but I continue to lock my fingers in between hers until we reach her back door.

She puts her hand on the knob after inserting and twisting

the key, unaffected by how drenched we are getting, and then looks over at me. A sadness dulls her eyes as she asks, "You believe me, don't you?"

I wet my bottom lip, tasting the rain. "Yes."

She nods once. "I'm sure you're hungry. Come in with me?"

"Are you offering to feed me?"

For a second, a smile crosses her lips. I didn't think I'd see one of those tonight, but it only makes the ache in my chest hurt more. "Would you turn it down?"

"No," I answer right away because I don't know if I could turn her down for anything at this point. Not while knowing our time is limited.

Satisfied, she turns the key and then the knob, and we head inside. Warmth folds around us, and I slip out of my wet jacket and drape it over the dining room chair. Next, I slide off my shoes at the same time as she kicks hers to the side.

"I don't have much," she says as she turns to the kitchen. "I haven't been grocery shopping in a few days, but-"

She stops dead in her tracks. I frown and fully face her backside. Her shoulders are stiff, and she's looking directly in front of her. Immediately, I get a tingle down the base of my spine, and it has nothing to do with how good her soaked backside looks and how it clings to every curve.

Her breath hitches. "Did you . . . Did you do that?"

"Do what?" I ask.

She moves aside and points toward her counter. "That?"

Resting on her counter is a flower.

One. Single. Lily.

My blood runs cold.

Memories surface, memories of how the same lily was left on my family's bodies. How they smelled when I bent, in rage and tears, to check them for a pulse even though I knew I wouldn't find one. The blood.

Before I know what I'm doing, I stomp my way through

the house to check the front door, only to find that it's locked, but as I back away from it, I notice the living room window slightly open. My nostrils flare as I head to it and slam it closed. I stand there for a moment, head bowed and fingers on the window's locks as memory after memory floods the back of my eyelids.

It's happening again. He has to know I'm in town. He has to be here. And he has to know I'm coming for him. Why else would he target Tori? Because that's exactly what that lily means.

"Killian?" Tori whispers from behind me. I hadn't heard her approach.

I shift my gaze over my shoulder, and when I find her holding the lily, I fully turn to face her, careful to keep the turmoil of emotions from my face.

"Is this what I think it is?" she asks quietly.

Flexing my jaw, I give a curt nod.

Her grip on the stem tightens, and I watch as she swallows thickly. Tears gather in her eyes. "Okay," she whispers, and it's then that I watch as realization crosses her face. She's being hunted, and now she knows it.

"Do your cameras reach the front?" I rumble softly as my gut bottoms out.

She shakes her head and sets the lily on the coffee table. "But you can see part of the front of the driveway."

"Let me look then."

"Okay," she squeaks, and together, we head to the dining room where her laptop rests.

She opens it, clicks a few buttons, and I come to stand beside her as she rights herself from her bent-over position. The camera plays through quickly on fast forward, and when movement comes across the screen, she slows it down. Her breath hitches as a man in an orange raincoat comes into the edges of the screen. In his hand is the lily.

Rage fills me. Rage like before. Rage reminiscent of back home before I left. It does not crest as we watch him leave, empty-handed, a few minutes later.

"Do you have anywhere you can stay?" I ask in a demanding way.

A single tear spills down her cheek as she answers, "With Tegan and Cole, but I don't want to burden them. I don't want them anywhere near this."

I can understand that, so I nod. There's no telling what this guy will do to get to her, and if she wants to keep her friends safe, she'll have to leave them out of it. "Then I'm staying in the house with you."

The way she nods is filled with relief, but still, more tears fall. I take her head in my hands, wipe her tears with my thumbs, and press my lips to her eyebrow. "I won't let anything happen to you."

"Okay," she manages thickly.

I pull away and look hard into her eyes. "No one will touch you." Because I won't make the same mistake twice. How he knew that I was close to Tori, I'll never know because I thought I'd been careful. But the only person who we suspect who knows that I've been spending time with her is the fucking pastor. Tori was right. Based on the camera feed, that man could have easily been him.

I could easily hunt down the pastor. I could easily rip answers from him, but we've already brought in the law. Before, I ran under the radar. But now? Now I have to play by the rules. Nothing pisses me off more.

"Come on," I whisper while hoping that I kept the anger from my tone. "Let's get you to bed."

I start to guide her toward the hallway but halt when she asks, "Sleep with me?"

She didn't know that I had already planned to because I'll be damned if I let her out of my sight now. Not until I find this guy. Not until he pays for what he's done and the threat he just delivered.

Instead of telling her all this, I murmur my agreement.

Chapter 23

Tori Townsend

A WARM BODY is snug against my back, but that's not what stirs me awake. It's not the morning songs from the birds nor the sun peeking through my curtains. What wakes me is a stiff cock against my ass and something cold making a trail from below my belly button to the edge of my hip.

The cold feels nice compared to the man's heat behind me, and I murmur an unintelligible and sleepy approval. He chuckles against my hair before biting my shoulder.

My tank top has ridden up my abdomen, and the straps are off my shoulders, but that cold continues to trail back and forth along my skin. Goosebumps rise over my flesh, and, curious enough to wonder what's causing them, I look down.

And then, I freeze.

The flat of the blade teases my skin, held by Killian's large hand. He rumbles a reassurance against my shoulder, and for a few seconds, I remain stiff.

"I could cut your fear away, dollface," he whispers in a tone so deep that I almost don't understand him. He trails the blade again, this time scraping against the skin. "Make you feel something else. Make you remember that you're alive and with me."

My breathing quickens the more he whispers, and I'd be lying if I said it didn't turn me on. I've been curious about pain since I started delivering it to him, wondering what it felt like and why it turned him on so much. The promises he's making me are attractive and teasing. My nipples harden at the way he whispers it, like it's a secret he's willing to share.

"But it'll hurt," I say.

"That's the point," he murmurs with a chuckle. "Do I have your consent to mark up this pretty skin? To mark the perfect curves?"

Biting my bottom lip, I turn to my back and look him in the eye. I find nothing but heat and security as he stares back at me, waiting for my answer. I can tell he wants this as much as I'm starting to.

Taking a leap of faith because I trust him with every part of me, I nod.

A smirk tucks into the edges of his lips, and he leans forward, taking my mouth. The blade continues to make little paths along my stomach, and I shiver when it pushes up my tank top a little further.

His tongue dives into my mouth, teasing my own, and I kiss him back as every sensitive part of me clenches with need.

One more pass of the blade by my ribs, and he applies pressure. Pain blossoms when he splits the skin, and I suck in a sharp breath from his mouth. He groans his approval at my sudden pain; like he'd been waiting forever for me to feel it.

At first, my mind rebels against it. It tells me that there's pain and that my fight or flight should kick in. But I shove it aside and turn the pain into something else. Something that makes my clit throb: pleasure. After all, pain and pleasure walk a fine line together, and I hadn't known how much until this very moment.

My fear about last night ebbs, crests, and then falls until all I feel is what he's doing to me. I moan into his mouth as he makes another slice across my ribs, loving the way it takes away all my internal pain, my crippling fear for my life. I can feel a warm wetness trickle down my outer ribs, and he breaks the kiss to watch it flow. For a second, his eyes flash with heat, and then he rubs his finger through it. I shouldn't be turned on by the way he examines the blood, the pure lust in his expression, but I am.

With one flick of his eyes to mine, he lifts himself until he's on his knees between my thighs and brings the blade to my thin shorts. I don't have time to ask him what he's doing when he pinches the hem with one hand and slices through them with the knife.

The blade knicks my skin, but I'm so turned on by how badly he wants my most sensitive area exposed to him that I feel nothing but arousal. He continues to cut until one thigh is free, then he moves to the other side. When my shorts are nothing but tatters, he pulls them away, exposing my pussy.

Wetting his bottom lip, he stares for a moment, taking in how wet I am, how much I like this, and how much I want more. The blade moves, and he touches my clit with the backside, and I moan at how it tickles, how cold and good it feels. He rubs it back and forth, and the sensation makes me squeeze my eyes shut to keep my shit together and not fall into a greedy, begging mess.

I feel him part my legs a little further, and then he pushes a rough finger inside me. My eyes fly open at the sudden intrusion, and then they flutter as he begins massaging my g-spot at the same time that the back of the knife continues to slide along my clit, rubbing the needy, throbbing bundle of nerves.

I grab the sheet beneath me and curl it into my palms. Heat coils in my lower abdomen because, not only does this feel amazing, but it's dangerous. At any moment, he could cause me serious harm, irreparable damage. Between the sensations and the trust and how fucking hot this is, I find myself close to cumming.

"Tell me how good it feels," he rumbles.

Through hooded eyes, I glance down, taking in the scene and how he watches my pussy with such intensity and heat that my nipples pebble further. "Please. Please don't stop."

He applies more pressure to the finger inside me, rubbing and fucking me with one single digit. The back of the blade slides faster along my clit, a sharp sting as he applies more pressure there too. My back bows off the bed while my head presses further into the pillow below it. A deep moan escapes my open mouth, and my breathing becomes hitched and labored. I work like hell to keep it together, to not cum so soon, and to enjoy the feeling of being pleasured, but my body has other ideas.

Heat spikes in my veins, and my lower abdomen explodes as I cum with a cry. My pussy ripples and tugs on his moving finger. Of their own accord, my legs twitch, and my toes curl, and it takes everything I have to remain where I am, clenching the sheets while my chest rises toward the ceiling.

"Hmm," he murmurs with approval as I come down from my high, a panting mess. I stare at the ceiling in disbelief that I came from a knife and an expert finger, so I don't notice it until the tip of his cock teases my entrance. I hadn't even heard nor felt him remove his pants because I'd been so occupied with the bliss.

In one smooth motion, his arm slides under my backside, and in the next moment, I'm flipped to my knees and elbows, my ass exposed to him. Anticipation builds, and I can feel his stare at my exposed, most sensitive areas.

The coldness of the blade starts at the middle of my back and trails down my spine to my puckered hole. I shiver involuntarily, but instead of using it to deliver more pain, he shoves his cock so deep in my pussy that I gasp. The knife falls away as he groans, and he remains seated there as my inner walls pulsate around his length.

Where the blade had moved across my skin is now being teased by his calloused hand. He starts at my puckered hole, circling it and teasing the sensitive flesh until he moves it upward along my spine, past my shoulders, and at the nape of my hair. And then his fingers curl, and he yanks on the roots. Pain and pleasure blaze within me, shooting electric bolts straight to my nipples. I moan at this new sensation and moan again when he starts to move within me.

"Always so fucking tight," he bites out.

My nipples brush against the sheet, hightening every-fucking-thing while he moves behind me. The bed bumps against the wall, and our mutual moans seem to time with it. The way he fucks me is just like his last name: completely savage. Punishing. Painful. Primal. It's like he can't get enough of my pussy. It makes me feel beautiful and wanted, and it only solidifies the fact that I can trust myself in the care of this man. Even with my flaws. My weight. My obvious, current issues.

He tightens his grip as he pounds into me, and I suck in a sharp breath at the further sting of pain. His grip is as strong and sure as the way he's fucking me. This powerful man behind me is delivering all the pain and pleasure I didn't know was possible. The way his length stretches me, the way his shaft rubs my g-spot, and the pain along my scalp that travels all the way down my spine and wraps around to my breasts.

"It's going to be hard to leave you," he confesses in a husky, breathy tone. His fingers splay before they take my hair again as if the thought is so painful that it hurts even his fingers.

"Then don't," I say just as breathlessly. Even to my own ears, I can't believe I said it. I don't cling to anyone. It's not in my nature. But here I am, asking him to stay. Wordlessly telling him not to leave me.

He says nothing in return, and as he continues to fuck me,

I wonder where his thoughts are heading. What he'd say if he weren't so damn guarded. What he'd promise me if he stripped away his painful layers and bared it all to me.

Heat coils in my abdomen despite where my thoughts have taken themselves. I start to gasp my moans as I crest closer and closer to an orgasm. He must know because he reaches around and pinches my clit between his thumb and pointer finger, and it's enough to send me crashing completely over the edge.

I cum with a moan so deep that it scratches at my throat.

"Fuck," he shouts, and with a few more pumps, he yanks himself out. He groans deeply as his cum covers my ass in ropes of wet warmth. And when he's finished, he releases my hair and leans to nibble on my spine. A few seconds later, he holds a towel that he gently uses to clean me up.

I flop over when he's done and watch as he tosses the towel by the bedroom door. Twisting my lips to the side, I contemplate whether I want to continue the conversation opener he started. It's a discussion I want to have but I know he won't give me. So instead of being direct, I say, "I meant what I said." He looks at me, and I prop myself on my elbows as I watch him cross the room back to the foot of the bed. His cock glistens in the morning light that's making its way through the crack between my curtains. I try like hell not to let it distract me as I continue, "I don't do this. You're the first man that's slept in my bed since I was in college."

He blinks at me, and I get the feeling that I'm inching dangerously close to the conversation he doesn't want to have. And I don't know why I do it, but I press my luck by adding with a tinge of humor, "Does this mean we're dating?"

Lifting his hand, his biceps bunching, he responds, "Dating would imply that I take you on dates."

I smile at him teasingly, knowing that I'm making him incredibly uncomfortable. "I count the field as a date."

He drops his hand back to his side and takes a deep breath

before saying, "I meant what I said, too. I'm not the marrying type."

I blink at the leap in the conversation, and the smile fades from my face. "I'm not either. I vowed I never would. It even terrifies me to have kids – I never want them. But no one said anything about marrying. There are plenty of people who don't marry and are together until the day they die."

I watch as he studies my face… and watch more intently as his gaze moves to the cuts he made on my ribs. For the second time tonight, I wonder where his thoughts are taking him. Like always, he's careful to keep them from his expression.

Crawling onto the bed, he takes a seat next to me, places his hands on his thighs, and curls his fingers against his flesh. "You remind me of her, you know," he mutters.

For a second, I hold my breath because I know that that nugget of information did not come easy. It gives me hope, and I know with Killian, this kind of hope will be fleeting. "Who?" I ask, even though I already have an inkling.

He looks over at me, square in the eyes. "My wife."

I swallow thickly at the intensity of his stare. "Is that a bad thing?" I ask because I need to know. I need to know if I'm hurting him or healing him.

He shakes his head a little. "No. You make me believe that there's a part of me that's no longer dead. Maybe that I can have more."

I can hear the 'but' in his tone, so instead of waiting for him to say it, I say it for him. "But you have to avenge her first."

When his lips thin and he nods, my heart breaks a little because I don't like to see him hurting, even if he's only barely showing it. "You don't have to do it alone, you know."

His brows furrow. "What?"

"I may not have known your wife, but I would never

tarnish her memory. I'll help you find this guy. No one said you have to do this alone."

He shakes his head again. "I won't put you in danger. You're too close to this already."

I touch his arm, and he glances at the contact. "You're here to protect me, remember?"

His throat bobs as he swallows, and I don't know if he believes it when he nods, but I take the tentativeness for what it is: a reluctant agreement.

And I'd be lying if I didn't say that the very idea of having more time with him only adds to my dangerous hope.

Chapter 24

Killian Savage

I SNAP my bracelet as I lean against a brick building across from Derek's thrift store. I watch the windows of his store, my reflection staring back. I debate whether I'm going in or not while thoughts of Tori circle in my head like a merry-go-round. Thoughts about her, thoughts about me and the kind of man I should be for her, and the fact that I don't know if I can be that man.

I look off into the distance with a flick of my eyes, past the boundaries of this little town. When I came here, I was a man without ties. Without passion aside from rage. I had nothing holding me back, not one goddamn thing, from making the Lillian pay. And now? Within more than a few days, I found myself tied down. I find myself with the desire to dig in roots, and it's all thanks to one woman.

How did she do it? I didn't even realize it until last night how much she'd wiggled her way past my hard exterior. Past my defenses. But she found a crack and pushed her way through. Maybe she made the crack herself. If she did, she did it without me looking.

Despite how many times I try to mend that crack, try to weld it closed, she remains. A constant thought in the back of my head. A smile on my lips. A dire need to tell her everything – all the dark and twisted things that make me who I am.

She represents a future I might possibly be able to have.

She said she's going to help me get my revenge, but does she know everything I have planned for him? Will she be able to stomach it? Would she hold the axe for me when I can no longer swing it?

And when it's over? When he's no longer breathing, could I just walk away from her and go back to my life like I'd planned? It was hard enough to turn my back on my family's graves, my heart and soul, just to do this. How can I do it a second time with Tori?

The door opens to the thrift store, and Derek pops his head out. I internally cringe when the wind catches his comb-over and makes it flutter in awkward ways.

Behind his glasses, his gaze immediately finds mine. A scowl crosses his face. From across the street, he shouts, "Are you just going to stare all day, or are you going to come in?"

I readjust the bracelet so it settles comfortably, and then I push off the wall to stride across the street. At first, I had considered walking away from what I'm about to buy, but the more I thought about Tori, the more I believed I needed it.

Tori left for work this morning, and it took everything in me to not go with her. To not hover at her store like a shadow in the corner. She reassured me that she wouldn't be alone, however, so I have to have faith that the Lillian won't do any of his bullshit with others around. That's not usually how he's done things, so I use that to tame my unease.

Derek steps outside to hold the door open for me, and I step in, breathing in the familiar scent of stale, used clothes.

"A beautiful day," he greets. "A rare one it would seem. Maybe it'll dry up all the ponds we seem to have grown."

"Sure."

"You don't give much away, do you?" he asks to my back.

"No," I answer.

"So, what will it be this time?" he asks as the door closes behind us. "Another outfit?"

Outfit. As if I'm here to dress in something new every day. He hasn't a fucking clue.

"No," I say in a deep voice, swiveling my gaze around the shop until I find a few cases along the wall. I start to make my way toward them.

I hear Derek's footfalls along the tile as he follows close behind me. I can practically feel his brimming questions when I reach them and bend to peer inside. "Is this all you have?"

I quickly glance at him, only to find him uncomfortably stuffing his hands into his pockets. "What – uh – what are you looking for?"

"A gun," I rumble.

Derek's eyebrows raise above his large glasses. "What could you possibly need a gun for?"

"Hunting," I answer simply, righting myself to a full standing position as I stare him down. It's not a complete lie. If the Lillian even tries anything, I'll pull the trigger. It'll be open season for bastards. Screw my drawn-out plan so he can feel every inch of pain that I've felt since the moment I stepped foot into my home. If I see him anywhere near Tori, I have no problem with ending his life before he can take her.

He clears his throat and rocks back on his heels. "I see. Mind if I ask what you're hunting for?"

"I mind."

"Right." He pinches his lips together as he considers me, and I know then and there that I'm going to have a fight getting my hands on one. "Should I be worried?"

I flex my jaw and flare my nostrils. "Do you have one or not?"

He sighs and glances at the case. "Those knives are the only thing you can buy here. I don't sell guns at my store, and you can't get one in Utah unless you're a resident."

My jaw clenches so hard that I'm surprised my teeth don't crack. That is not what I wanted to hear, and my gut drops in utter disappointment that curls with a sliver of fear. "Do you have a gun I can borrow?"

His gaze snaps to mine. "No," he spits. "I don't like guns."

"Do you know anyone who does?"

His lips thin into a fine line, and he carefully says, "I get the feeling you're not hunting for anything with four legs for a pelt you can throw over your shoulders."

"What I need it for is none of your concern."

Without looking at it, he taps the glass case's surface. "A knife is all I can sell you. Take it or leave it."

"Fine," I bite out. It's not what I want, but it'll have to do. Somehow. I point to the case at one particular knife and add, "I'll take that one."

Wordlessly, he travels to the other side of the case, grabs a set of keys from his pocket, and inserts it into the lock. The lock clicks, and he slides the glass door open. He carefully picks up the knife by the hilt and takes it to the register. I follow him while digging money out of my pocket.

As he rings me up, he grumbles, "You know I'll have to report this to the sheriff, right?"

I don't answer him and pass him the money instead. I know that, legally, he doesn't have to. He'd do it to relieve his conscience.

He hands me the bag with the knife inside. "You're trouble, Killian. I can smell it."

"Then take a big whiff," I murmur angrily. With the bag in my hand, I walk out of the store.

Chapter 25

Tori Townsend

I'M a little late opening the shop this morning. I hadn't planned to be late, but between my time with Killian and errands, I arrived later than planned.

I park the car in my usual spot and quickly shut off the engine. Grabbing my things, I then dash from the car and to the front door. Thankfully, there are no customers waiting to get in, and as I insert the key to the shop, I take a calming breath.

That calming breath is momentary, however, because footsteps coming in my direction cause me to look up, and then promptly feel a tinge of fear.

"Tori," Kent greets with a raised upper lip, as though I stink and the very thought of being in my space causes him discomfort. I know I don't smell. I showered with Killian before I left the house. Kent is just being an asshole, and even though I know that, I still can't shake the fear as he comes to stand before me.

He left that lily. I know he did. And now he has the

audacity to stand before me as if he hadn't broken into my house to give me, at the very least, a warning.

I back up a step, the key in the door dangling and all but forgotten, and that only makes him smile.

"Kent," I greet in a shaky voice. Suddenly, I'm fully aware of the clouds, of the sounds of birds, and of the smell of freshly cut grass. If he takes me now, no one would know. "I'll scream," I threaten.

His expression remains the same as he says, "Is that supposed to matter to me?"

A car passes by, and for a brief moment, I want to beg them to stay. "If you try to take me, they'll know who to look for."

He cocks his head to the side. "Whatever do you mean? Take you? Where would I take you, Tori?"

In this moment, I wish like hell Killian was here. I shouldn't have reassured him that I'd be fine, but at the same time, I didn't know I'd be so openly confronted in broad daylight where anyone could see. I thought I'd be kidnapped in the dark somewhere. Scratch that; I didn't actually think I'd ever be kidnapped. It was in my mind, but denial is a funny thing.

"I know it was you," I whisper.

"Me?"

"Yes, you. You're the one who chased that woman onto the street – the woman I hit. You kidnapped Susan Toro." I swallow thickly. "You broke into my house and left me the lily."

He crosses his arms and looks at me like I'm a child making the wrong choices. "Why would you think that? That's a horrible thing to accuse me of."

Anger rises in me because he's basically calling me a liar. I *know* it was him who did all those things. I know it's him working for the Lillian. Kent may not be breeding the women he takes, but he's on board with all of it, and he's certainly aiding the one who is.

"I'm not stupid," I mutter. I hate that I feel small in front of him. Vulnerable. But he's always been a shark. He's always been out for blood when it comes to me. Hell, when it comes to anyone who views the world differently than his perfect and pure ideal world, he attacks.

"No one would be surprised if you were."

A tendril of anger licks at my insides. It's because of him that I barely have any business. I already know how he feels about me. However, every time he brings it up, I feel even smaller.

With my purse's strap tucked tightly in my elbow, I cross my arms loosely over my chest. "What do you want, Kent?"

He waves a hand gently around, ever the icon of grace. "I was just going for a stroll. It's a rare sunny morning." His tone makes my skin crawl because that definitely wasn't what he was doing. Most likely, he saw me pull up, and he wanted to see how rattled I was. Well, mission accomplished. I want nothing more than to flee like a damn deer.

By now, I know what Josiah's car sounds like. The engine grumbles as the breaks squeal, and I feel relief as he parks the car right in front of us. Kent certainly can't take me now. Thank god for employees – and on-time ones at that.

"Goodbye, Kent," I say with more vigor than I feel.

Josiah hops out of the car and takes in the two of us; Kent's easygoing demeanor and my stiff one. He approaches cautiously. "Everything okay?" he asks.

"Oh, just fine," the man of god says cheerfully as if we are really neighbors who actually get along.

"He was just leaving," I add. Now that Josiah is here, I feel more in control. I step into Kent's space, turn the key, and push the door open, effectively dismissing the pastor.

"I'll see you again, Tori," he calls as I step fully inside my shop with Josiah right behind me. I halt in my next step because the hair on the back of my neck stands on end. It sounded like a threat, and it probably was.

The door shuts, effectively stamping out Kent from my immediate life, and I give myself a little shake as I head to the light switch and flick on all the lights.

"Did I miss something?" Josiah asks as he follows me to the counter.

I head to the register and blow out a breath. "Nope," I respond because, even though that pastor may trash-talk me, I try to make it a habit not to air my dirty laundry. I find it just gives him fuel for harassment.

On the other hand, maybe I should tell Josiah. I glance at him, only to find him watching me with curiosity. He must know I'm lying. If I told him, he'd be a witness of sorts when Kent finally does what he's threatened and takes me.

That makes me want to throw up.

Instead of dwelling on it, however, I take a deep breath and plaster on a fake smile. "Thanks for being on time today."

He nods and slowly, my smile becomes real, because I truly am grateful for him.

I give him a list of things to do while I head to the office and begin my tasks for the day, chiefly getting my desk in order. It doesn't take long before a knock sounds on my door.

Solely into my sore store's budget on my laptop, I glance up distractedly. Tegan stands there, a bag of donuts in one hand and a coffee in her other.

I lean back in my seat as she dips inside and passes me both the coffee and the bag. "I thought I told you no more donuts."

"When we're sad, we feed each other sugar," she says in the way of explanation.

"Mhmm," I hum, opening the bag and taking a whiff of my favorite morning pastry.

She takes a seat in the chair and props her feet on the coffee table as she sips from her own coffee cup. No doubt it's decaf. I have every faith that she's taking care of her body in the way that she's supposed to while pregnant.

A gentle hand rests on her lower abdomen while she watches me closely. And when I set the bag of donuts down on the desk without pulling out my breakfast, she scowls. "What's wrong?"

I only flick my gaze at her. "Nothing," I lie.

She rolls her eyes. "Not this again. Come on, Tori. What's wrong?"

I shake my head as I fight the lump in my throat.

Her feet slide back down to the floor and she leans in my direction. "Did they find out anything else about the woman with the brand? Is that what's wrong?"

I shake my head again. "No, I haven't heard anything on that."

"Then what is it?"

Using both hands, I scrub my cheeks with my palms. I could keep her in the dark. I could lie to protect her. But I tell her everything. She knows every part of my life, and if I break that now . . . what kind of friend would I be? What kind of friendship would we have if I suddenly went missing and she never saw me again?

So, I tell her. I tell her about the orange raincoat, the harassment of the pastor, the lilies he plucked from the field, the woman kidnapped in the same town where he works, and all the way to the flower left on my counter. Then I tell her about Killian and his ties with the Lillian and how every piece of the puzzle connects to one another.

She listens silently, but expressions flick across her face. Shock, sadness, anger. They flit back and forth as my story goes on, and when I'm finished, she simply stares at me.

"Say something," I whisper when the silence becomes too much. "I can't stand the silence."

"I could have Cole murder him," she suggests with

complete seriousness. "Then he wouldn't be a problem anymore."

I run a hand through my hair and lean once more into the back of my chair. "Tempting. That would just cause more problems though."

"It's better than you being taken to be bred like cattle. It's more than tempting, and you know it."

"Yeah," I breathe. "But Killian won't let that happen."

"Killian can't be around all the time, Tori," she whispers.

I look down at my palms. "Yeah," I say again. "I know."

"Does Pierce know?"

I close my fists, and annoyance curls in my gut. "Some of it. I haven't told him about the lily though."

She sips from her coffee again. "You should. He might change his tune if he knew someone broke into your house, lily aside."

I consider this for a moment. Pierce may have shut both Killian and me down once, but he can't deny a break-in. I should tell him. I should do something about it, if for no other reason than to let the authorities know that I'm being targeted. That I could be next, right along with Susan Toro. The thought should comfort me, but it doesn't because, from what Killian says, the Lillian will go to great lengths to get the woman he targets.

I just hope that, with Killian around, with people constantly around me, he won't be able to. Unless . . . he decides to hurt them to get to me. After all, he did kill Killian's family in revenge. He could easily kill one of the people I care about, someone I love.

I look back at Tegan, who watches me and waits for my answer. He could hurt her, and the best way I can keep that from happening is to tell Pierce so he can start an investigation. With any luck, It'll give him the evidence he needs to start to question the man who raised him.

"You're right," I say, and then I pick up my phone.

Chapter 26

Killian Savage

AS SOON AS the rest of the officers leave out her front door, Pierce stands in the living room with us, rubbing the back of his neck as if all the weight of the world had settled there. They've been here for an hour, scouring the place for any evidence that might have been left behind from the break-in.

I had come back from the thrift store only to find Tori home and three police cars parked out front. After stashing my newly acquired knife in the B&B, I made my way to the house to see what was going on. Tori had ended up calling them about the break-in, and while at first, she was micro-managing, she sat on the couch after my reassurance, chewing her nails while staring at the lily in one of the officer's clear evidence bags.

"Well?" Tori asks around biting a nail down so far that I'm surprised it doesn't bleed. I stand to the right of her knees, fighting the urge to pull her hand out of her mouth. I understand it though, even if we're both nervous for different reasons. I don't like cops for obvious reasons, and I couldn't relax enough to sit next to her with the fresh reminder of the break-in. So I just hovered nearby the entire time instead. Besides, I think that's what she needed, a pillar of protection against what horrors and truths Pierce and his guys might have found.

Pierce drops his hand back to his side and fully turns to face her. "There were no prints aside from yours and his." He tips his head to me and sighs but continues, "Whoever it was must have worn gloves."

"You found nothing?" I demand in disbelief, though I shouldn't be disbelieving. When I reported my family's bodies, they hadn't found any evidence either.

"The window wasn't tampered with. It had been unlocked to begin with. There's nothing more to say."

I can hear it in his tone, the accusation toward Tori for being irresponsible. It makes my shoulders tighten, but I keep my mouth shut because what I really want to say and do could land me a night in jail. There, I wouldn't be able to protect her.

"And the cameras?" Tori presses.

He shakes his head and crosses his arms. "There's nothing there but the orange coat. Nothing to go on."

"That man's body had the same shape as Kent's," she growls, lowering her fingers from her mouth and bunching them into fists against her knees.

"Not this again."

"When will you believe me?" she all but shouts.

"When you have actual evidence, Tori," he says patiently.

"Well, I suppose I should tell you about today, then."

Before he can protest any more bullshit from his mouth, she starts to recount an interaction she had with the pastor this morning. My blood runs hot. Then it turns ice cold because, if that kid employee of hers hadn't shown up, there's no telling what could have happened. Fear nearly makes me sit down next to her, almost has me collapsing onto the couch, because I had let her go alone. I knew better, and I let her go anyway.

Their conversation draws me back to the present even though my mind wants to dwell on all the possible ways I could have lost her forever.

"Why else would he have said what he said? Acted the way he acted?" Tori asks when Pierce only considers her and the situation carefully.

"If you do nothing and something happens…" I let my words trail off, knowing that he has to choose between investigating his grandfather to get to the Lillian and having a guilty conscience if something else were to happen to her.

Pierce rakes a hand down his face. "I'll see about a search warrant."

"If he's not guilty," Tori spits, "Then he'll let his grandson in his house to have a look around, now won't he."

"I still have to go about this the legal way."

I roll my eyes. If he wanted to go about this the legal way, he would have looked at his grandfather several days ago.

"Something to say, Savage?" Pierce directs at me in a threatening manner.

"Oh, I have plenty to say." I take a step in his direction, letting the rage fuel my motions. I can't protect her to my full capability if even the law won't stand behind her.

"Stop," Tori interjects. "Stop!"

Pierce's narrowed eyes relax when he looks back at Tori. I nearly chuckle darkly because, even after all the shit they've been through the last few days, everything she's slung at him, he still has it bad for her. Color me territorial red.

She continues, "I'd also like a restraining order against him."

It takes a minute, but Pierce curtly nods. "I'll do what I can. And though I don't think he's who you're looking for –"

She chuffs. "You're in such denial," she interjects.

"– I agree that he has it out for you."

She shakes her head, opens her palms, and flexes her fingers into her palms a few times. "Whatever," she whispers. "Just please do your job."

Pierce sighs long and slow, but he says nothing else before grabbing the door handle and exiting the house, leaving me and Tori alone.

Sagging her shoulders, she looks up at me. "I want nothing more than to move."

I shrug a little. "I can help with that."

She laughs softly, but the sound has very little humor in it. "Tempting." Standing, she gathers herself to her toes and tucks her head under my chin. She breathes out contentedly as if she'd been waiting for comfort since the moment I stepped into her house. I wrap an arm around her and kiss the top of her head while my eyes go out to her sunny front lawn.

"Better?" I ask after a few moments.

"I will be once there's a restraining order."

I almost huff, but I stop myself because no law and order will stop the Lillian from taking his mark. Nothing will stop him from showing me he can, either. And, truth be told, even if that restraining order doesn't come through, I'll find where the pastor lives myself and watch him bleed until he tells me what I want to know. Until he's good and dead inside a house fire for what he's done to Tori, too.

Because I know he has answers. And I know he has to pay.

I have every intention of doing that.

Chapter 27

Tori Townsend

"YOU'RE VIBRATING," Killian murmurs as I stand up from the water of the bathtub. Water slooshes off me and makes trickling sounds as it meets the surface of the bathwater. The bath was his idea in hopes that it would calm the nerves and anxiety that had taken over my body since the moment that lily was found. It worked for a while, while the water was scolding hot and I was under his watchful eye. Now, he's leaning against the vanity, arms crossed as he scans my body with a hungry gaze that he tries so damn hard to hide.

"I'm cold," I murmur back, knowing full well that that's a lie. It even tastes bitter on my tongue.

Reaching beside him, he grabs the folded towel, snaps it free, and heads to me. Gently, he starts drying me, and after a moment of silence, of letting that lie linger between us, he says, "It's more than that."

I look in the mirror across from me as he bends down and dries my legs. My eyes look wild and yet so empty. Fear will do that, I guess. Kent stole that from me, my sense of comfort.

The only time I feel comfort and protection is when I'm in Killian's arms. I practically crave it these days, need it like air. Why does that make me feel guilty?

He must notice me watching myself because he turns me from my reflection and backs me to the vanity. Resting the damp towel over his shoulder, he lifts me enough to sit me on the edge. "He won't touch you," he whispers.

"You can't be there all the time, Killian," I say just as quietly.

Taking my chin, he makes me meet his eyes. I search their depths and find nothing but sincerity as he responds, "I have nowhere else to be."

Butterflies flutter in my stomach, and my heart skips a little beat. "I can't ask that of you."

"I won't force it, but someone will be with you at all times. I won't accept anything less."

Biting my bottom lip, I give a small nod. He talked to me about this on the way to the bathroom and made me promise to keep my word. I don't plan to break that promise, and though he can't hover by me at work, I had already texted Tegan to meet me at the store in the morning so that I could make good on my promise.

"Good," he says before he takes my mouth in a tender kiss. I never knew such a big man could be so gentle, but he proves me wrong every time his lips lock with mine. It makes my blood sing, and I gave up a long time ago trying to make that feeling disappear. I'm no longer scared of what Killian offers, even if it is only temporary. I hope that it's not temporary, but I won't get my hopes up on believing that he'll stay. *For me.*

He grabs the base of my hair and tips my head to the side, exposing my neck. The stubble of his five-o'clock shadow tickles my skin as he peppers kisses from the point of my jaw down to my collarbone.

"What are you doing?" I ask as he goes even lower to the swell of my breast.

"Relaxing you," he rumbles against my skin. I shiver as goosebumps rise from the vibration of his voice and the heat from his mouth.

I tip my head back when his lips surround my nipple and his tongue flicks against the tight bud. A small sigh escapes me, and I tangle my hands in his hair to keep him there. His tongue swirls and teases, and every now and then, he nips. Soon, my quicker breath becomes moans and I start pushing him further down my body.

He chuckles as he bends, knowing exactly what I want, what I need. Resting himself on his knees, he looks up at me and spreads my thighs. His nostrils flare a little as he inhales. "You smell so damn good." And then his eyes move to my pussy, and the heat that flashes in them makes the same heat pool in my lower abdomen.

I tremble, and this time it's for an entirely different reason than fear. Here, with him, with the way he's looking at me, all that fear melts away. The moment is all that matters.

He leans forward and brushes his tongue against my clit, and the sight of him between my legs is almost too much to bear. My legs start to push against his hands, my thighs always desperate to keep him there by locking his head in place. His grip remains firm, however, and his fingers dig into the thick flesh as a small but totally hot punishment.

My hand finds his hair again, and I give a tug on the roots when he sucks my clit into his mouth. He hums against me, and I sharply inhale a deep breath at the sudden sensation. With my clit in his mouth, he slowly swirls his tongue around the tip. I quiver around him, and it shakes the vanity. "Oh my god," I breathe out. A moan quickly follows. "P-p-please don't stop."

The heat in my lower abdomen intensifies as he starts pulsing his sucking motions at the same time his tongue swirls.

He opens my legs even wider, burying himself fully between my legs as he feasts. I can't help but watch and solely give in to everything his gifting me.

My other hand skates up my curvier stomach until it finds the breast that never got attention. I squeeze before I start pinching the nipple. My mouth opens at this added pleasure, and I can't help but breathe through my mouth because my inhales and exhales have become so ragged.

Using his shoulder to keep my thigh where he wants it, he moves his hand to my entrance and slowly inserts a finger. I gasp at the intrusion, my eyes flying wide, and then he crooks his finger and begins massaging my g-spot. My groan is so loud that, if someone were in the living room, they'd definitely know what we are doing by now.

Then he adds another finger, pumps, and stretches.

And then he adds one more.

The heat coils and tightens until it bursts, and I cum with a moan so deep that it scratches at my throat. My thighs shake around his head, and his fingers are slick with my cum, but he doesn't let up. He continues to ride it out with me. Pulsing his tongue against my clit. Massaging my g-spot, fingers digging into my thigh.

When I'm finished, I slump against the mirror.

Slowly, he pulls out his fingers and removes his mouth from my clit. My juices coat his face, and I weakly lift the towel to give to him. He takes it as he rises to his feet, swiping away the wetness.

"Take off your pants," I all but demand in a heated tone.

He shakes his head.

"No?"

"Not tonight," he says. He tucks his hands underneath my armpits and lifts me off the vanity, setting me on my feet.

"Why not?" I pout up at him.

He raises his eyebrows. "You need sleep."

"But-"

He cuts me off with another shake of his head. "Come on." Taking my hand, he guides me out of the bathroom and to my bedroom. He doesn't bother turning on the lights as we head to the bed. In a mere few seconds, he's flipping back the covers and patting the mattress. I flatten my lips together as I crawl in dutifully and then sigh as warmth surrounds me when he covers me back up.

I watch in the darkness as he strips out of his shirt and pants, leaving only his underwear on. The shadows highlight his abs, and my mouth instantly waters, but I'll respect his wishes about solely taking care of my needs tonight. It truly is a sweet notion now that I've considered it.

He makes his way around the other side of the bed and crawls in beside me. Gathering me in his arms, he rolls onto his back and tucks my head under his chin, and god damn it, I nearly melt.

We stay there like that for a while, listening to the nothingness, both of us lost in thought. I don't know what he's thinking, but all I'm thinking about as I drift toward the edge of sleep is how safe I feel at this moment. How much I never want it to end. How I want to extend it for the rest of my life.

And when my eyes finally close and sleep pulls me under, I whisper against his chest, "I think I love you."

The only answer I get before I'm completely pulled under is his hand rising to my scalp to massage.

Chapter 28

Tori Townsend

"REAL SMOOTH, TORI," I grumble to myself in the parking lot of my shop. Tegan hasn't arrived yet, nor has she answered my text messages asking where she's at. She's probably driving. I know she doesn't like to text and drive, her parents having drilled that into her, and even though they're gone, the habit remains.

As I sit here, I berate myself. I cannot believe that I told Killian I loved him. I told myself I'd never let that happen again – never be vulnerable again – but he managed to make me fall for him without even trying. And the worst part? He didn't say anything back. If he did, I wasn't awake for it, which means it doesn't count, but I doubt he did. He's not going to confess any sort of feelings for me if he hasn't yet.

I raise my hand and press it to my forehead as the rain beats against my windows. Oh god, what if he doesn't even feel something for me aside from attraction? What if I'm just a wanted distraction? The thought hadn't occurred to me until now when I'm feeling all these feelings I told myself I'd never have again.

"You're a fucking idiot," I tell myself through gritted teeth. I release my forehead and shut off my borrowed car with more force than necessary. What the hell am I going to do now?

But he didn't disappear when you confessed, a little voice says in the back of my mind. He was still there when I woke up, and I was still wrapped in his arms. He was sleeping when I tiptoed out in shame to head to work, but the point is, he never left.

Why does he feel the need to protect me otherwise? It can't be because he feels guilty that this Lillian guy is after me. Can it? I have to believe it's more than that. I have to believe that he isn't just fucking me to pass the time until he can get his hands on him. It has to be more, but even if that's the case, will he ever confess how he feels for me before he up and disappears from my life?

I groan. I have it bad, and I know it.

Grabbing my phone from the cupholder, I check for messages from Tegan. There are no notifications, and it's well past opening hour, so, with a deep sigh, I decide to just open the damn shop myself. It breaks my promise to Killian, but at this point, I'm not even sure that Tegan is awake.

I pluck my purse from the passenger seat, drop the car keys and my phone inside, and exit the car. It's not like I need my phone anyway. Tegan will show when she shows. Hopefully, she brings coffee and breakfast to make up for being so late. Maybe then I'll forgive her for this walk I'm making alone.

My strides are small and distracted as I dig around inside the depths of my purse for the store keys, moving around my wallet. Frustrated for more than one reason, I shove aside all the other things that I never use but think I have to have with me at all times anyway.

A car pulls up into the parking lot, and I breathe a sigh of relief as I continue my search for the damn keys. "You better have breakfast," I murmur to Tegan even though she can't hear me inside the car.

I growl a little when my hand swipes against an open tube of chapstick. Honestly, why do I have all this stuff in here? Their combined weight only serves to give me shoulder pain.

The car door opens, but the car remains idling. When my fingers fumble against the store keys, I grasp them with excitement and take them out. I'm just about to hold them up in victory for Tegan to see, but a body presses against my back, and I'm shoved against the window of my store. My purse and keys drop and an arm clad in a slick, orange sleeve comes into view before a black sack is slid over my head.

I start screaming, my heart pounding, and when I'm picked up from behind, I begin to kick wildly. But it's no use because whoever has me is much stronger than I am.

"Kent!" I shout as he stomps his way back to the running car with me tight in his arms. "Let me go!" I kick wildly again and receive an 'oof' when I connect with a shin. "Let me go!"

I hear no answer from him. None whatsoever, but I should have expected that. I should have expected him not to listen, not even to the restraining order that his grandson should have delivered by now, but even as we get nearer to the running car, a part of me hopes he just drops me and leaves me.

My next scream rings in my ears when I'm tossed into the car, landing roughly on nothing but a hard metal floor. It's then I realize that this isn't a normal car. This . . . this is a van. A van with no seats in the back.

Kent crawls in after me, and I start throwing my hands around, hoping to connect with his head and knock him out. He grabs hold of both wrists with one hand of his own, and in the next second, they're tied together with the zip of zip ties.

Despite my best efforts to keep my legs from being tied next, it still happens. I'm out-matched, out-strengthed, and when the van's door shuts, I start to sob because I know nothing will stop him from taking me to the Lillian now.

Chapter 29

Killian Savage

DEREK IS quiet as we make our way to Mount Pleasant. He keeps looking over at me where I sit in the passenger seat of his truck, and I know he has a lot of things he wants to say, maybe even ask, but so far, he's refrained.

I asked him for a ride. He wanted to know why I had to go see Tori so desperately, but like usual, I gave him nothing. It's none of his damn business that I feel the need to explain myself to Tori. That I know she knows I said nothing back after she confessed her true feelings for me. All I did was pet her fucking head because I couldn't say the words. The last time I said them was to my wife before I left for a job, and the next time I saw her, she was dead.

I have to explain that to Tori, and I have to tell her that I'm all confused in my head and feeling things I can't quite explain. Things that I've closed myself off to and can't quite name anymore. The last thing I want is to have her walk away from me because I couldn't explain myself. The thought doesn't settle well with me. I'm not sure how much explaining

I'll be able to do, but I have to give her something. If her sneaking out this morning is anything to go by, she's upset about it.

"So," Derek begins, drawing out the word and making me cringe. My hopes for a silent ride dash. "How was – uh – how did your hunting go?"

"Haven't done it yet," I respond, keeping my eyes on the road – or what I can see of it past the ribbons of rain.

"Are you going to finally tell me what you're hunting?"

I glance at him. "No, because all you'll do is report it to your sheriff, right?"

He scowls. "I haven't told him anything yet. I'm still deciding if I need to."

"You don't."

"Then give me a reason not to."

I look back at the road, flexing my jaw, and give him absolutely nothing because, again, it's none of his business.

"Look," he sighs out. "This town talks quite a bit. Everyone sees everything, and everyone hears everything. Ever since Tori hit that woman, things have been off and none of it is adding up. I get the feeling that you know exactly what's going on."

I flick my eyebrows into my forehead, my only indication to him that he's correct.

"Care to share what the hell is going on?"

I give a quick shake of my head. "It'll be over with soon, so there's no need to worry about it."

He's quiet for a beat as we pull into Mount Pleasant's downtown. A few people are milling about with umbrellas and store lights on to make up for the lack of sun, but for the most part, it's seemingly empty everywhere we look. "Does it have anything to do with needing a gun?"

I say nothing again aside from breathing a sigh of relief when I see Tori's car outside her shop.

"Fine," he grumbles. He pulls into a parking space next

to Tori. "But I will eventually find out. The sheriff and I are on good terms. The news will get back to me at some point."

"Mhmm," I mumble as I grasp the door handle and open the cab to the rain. "Good luck with that." Because even the sheriff doesn't know the whole story. He only knows what I gave him, which was just enough for him to track down a lead and enough to finally get him to provide some sort of protection for Tori.

I step out into the rain, shut the truck's door, and turn toward the shop. As Derek backs out, I take a step forward. Rain pelts my jacket and soaks my hair as I fiddle with the bracelet and try to come up with some sort of wording for what I need to say to her.

I growl under my breath when I come up with nothing that would make sense and decide to just try anyway. She knows me well enough to know this sort of topic is hard for me.

My boots slosh in the puddles when I stride toward the shop's door. As soon as I open it, the cooler air seeps into my wet face and scalp, but I shake off the droplets before fully entering.

Tegan looks up from behind the counter with a frown on her face. It is still early, so she probably wasn't expecting any customers at this hour, but as soon as she sees me, her face relaxes.

"Hey," she greets cheerfully. "What are you doing here? Oh shit, did you come to see me?" She pauses and cocks a hip as she seems to gather some sort of courage. "I won't tell you any secrets about Tori. You're going to have to find those out yourself."

I frown and begin crossing the shop to her. "No," I rumble. "I came to see her."

Her frown matches my own. "Oh. Well, you can't."

"Why?" I say through gritted teeth. Did she tell her friend

to not let me through? Is she really that mad that I couldn't say it back?

"Geez," Tegan hisses, holding up her hands in surrender. "No need to get pissy. She's not here, Romeo. I don't know where she is."

I glance back at the windows to make sure that the car parked there is actually the car she's borrowed. When I see that it is, I turn back toward Tegan. "What do you mean? Call her."

Tegan cringes. "I found her purse by the front door. And the keys." She grabs something from under the counter, and then a purse appears on the surface. "Maybe she's at the hardware store?"

A sinking feeling settles in the pit of my gut. "You weren't here when she got here?"

She looks down at the purse with a guilty expression. "I overslept."

The sinking feeling intensifies until all I want to do is throw up. "Do you have cameras?"

Her head snaps up, and she meets my gaze once more. "Yeah, why?"

"Show me where they are," I demand.

"I don't think-"

"Tegan," I draw out the word, leaning forward and calmly splaying my hands on the counter. "Show me the cameras."

Her shoulders sag when she sighs. "Fine, but if this gets me into trouble, I'm going to tell everyone that you forced me to." As she walks around the counter and toward the back office, I hear her murmur under her breath, "Cole is going to kill me for being in the same room as this dude."

She opens the office door and flicks on the lights, and together, we head to the laptop resting on the desk. I swear to god, she's moving at a snail's pace, and it takes everything in me to not shove a pregnant woman aside and do it myself.

Calmly, as if she has no idea the direness of the situation, she takes a seat and swipes her finger across the mouse pad. I clench and unclench my fingers into fists as she types in the password and brings up the camera feed.

"I don't know what you're looking for."

"Show me when she arrived."

"Okay . . ." she mutters. She doesn't argue any further and backs the camera up until it picks up her parking the car in front of the store. She sits there for a while, checking her phone and muttering to herself, and then she climbs out and heads to the shop.

What happens next makes my breath stop. A black van pulls up. She doesn't notice.

As soon as a man in an orange raincoat steps out of the passenger side and slams Tori into the window, Tegan gasps. "What the hell is happening?" she demands.

I remain silent, my jaw clenched so hard that I'm surprised my teeth haven't shattered. Every nerve in my body is on fire, and every blood cell is ice-cold.

"Kent," I growl out. I can't see his face because of the hood, but I know it's him. No one else would have the balls to do this.

"Oh my god," she whispers as Kent picks her up and starts carrying her to the van. As soon as she's tossed inside and the door shuts, I'm moving away from the desk.

"Wait!" Tegan shouts. I pause in my step. "Look!"

Begrudgingly, because I know exactly what I'm going to do next, I turn back toward the laptop. Her finger is touching the driver's side of the van. Another man is sitting in it, wearing an orange raincoat, but his hood is down, and his face is as clear as day.

"What the fuck?"

"If that's Kent," she says, pulling her finger back to point at the other guy. "Who is that?"

"The Lillian," I spit.

"The Lillian? Wait! Where are you going?" she squeaks as I stomp my way to the door.

"To go find a sheriff and have a little chat about his grandfather," I say so deeply that my tonsils rattle.

And then I'm out the door, Tori's car keys in my hand with every fucking intention of making Pierce pay for not protecting my girl. I start the car with more force than necessary.

Chapter 30

Tori Townsend

WHATEVER I'M LYING on when the world starts to fade back into existence is not as soft as it should be. Situated on my side, I can feel the springs dig into my ribs. This mattress was designed to be uncomfortable, or it's just that old, and I groan as I shift around a little to try and relieve some of the ache in my side.

I remember everything: the rain, the blur of an orange raincoat, the bag over my head. *Kent.* He took me from my shop, and before he peeled out of the parking lot, he jabbed my arm with a needle.

Anything after that? I don't remember.

My head swims with emotions I can't quite touch because of the lasting effects of whatever drug he gave me. I have yet to open my eyes, however. I know that wherever he took me, I'm now a prisoner, and I don't want to see what my conditions will be.

My surroundings smell like mildew and the musty stench of damp stone. Somewhere outside, I hear a rooster and clucking chickens, and above me, I hear the pitter-patter of tiny feet racing around the floor. But it's when I hear whispers that my eyes slowly slide open because they're whispers of women, women muttering in fear.

"Tori?" a slightly familiar voice whispers to me.

Still resting on the mattress, I swivel my head toward the voice and find Susan next to me. I don't know what I expected. Bars maybe? Cages? Padded rooms? I knew the Lillian's women wouldn't be free to roam around. What I didn't expect was for none of those things to be true.

My gaze moves to Susan. Her slim face is dirty, and her red hair is a ratted mess. Beneath her rests her own mattress. It's soiled and stained, and the blanket she must be allowed is draped over her chest and around her arms.

She rests against a stone wall, and embedded in it is a chain that reaches to her legs and cuffs around her ankle.

I hear more murmurs and squint into the dimness to find two more women on the opposite wall. Their eyes are wide, and their blankets are swathed around their swollen, pregnant bellies.

This time, the fear does seep through the lasting effects of the drugs. Reality strikes true, and when it does, I sit up. My ankle veers in the opposite direction as my own chain tugs against my movements. "No," I whisper, wrapping my hand around the chain and giving it a yank. "No, this can't be happening."

Wildly, I search my surroundings. By the stone walls and the egress windows, I can tell that we're in a basement, and by the sounds of the outdoors, we're on a farm in god knows where.

My heartbeat slams against my ribs. The woman I hit comes fully to the front, the missing teeth, the burned-off fingerprints. It hits me then why the Lillian did that – to hide their identity if we were to escape. But a quick check of myself makes me calm just a smidge because my fingertips aren't burnt and my teeth are still there.

Despite that little fact of being unharmed, I scramble to my feet because I spot a window right next to me. My head is fuzzy, and I sway before I catch my balance on the stone. It scrapes my palm a little, but I don't truly notice as I shuffle my way to the window. The window is small, and even if I were to break free of my chain, I'd never fit through it.

Even though the pane is slightly dirty, I take in the outdoors. Chickens of all colors roam freely, and there are a few trees, a shed, and a barn, but in the distance, I can see the mountains underneath the darkness of the rain clouds.

I squint as I try to take in what's between me and the mountain. I can barely make out a main road and the red car that drives on it. It passes by white blobs, and I gasp as I come to realize what, exactly, those white blobs are.

"The field of lilies," I whisper as I splay my hand across the dirty glass. How fucking fitting that the Lillian lives next to a patch of lilies.

"What?" Susan whispers back.

We both look up as children giggle from above, the Lillian's children. These women's children. I swallow thickly and return my gaze to hers. "We aren't far from town."

That gives me hope where, in a place like this, hope doesn't exist. At least, not for these women, but if we're this close, we shouldn't be so hard to find.

That is… if anyone is looking for us. *For me.*

They hadn't been able to find where the woman I hit came from. Even if they saw the cameras, they wouldn't know where to look for me.

Tears threaten to prick my eyes as I succumb to my fate. I head back to my mattress, slump down on the springs, and bury my face in my hands. I'm going to end up just like these women, pregnant against my will, a prisoner, pumping out children for a sick and twisted man.

Chains rattle before a hand comes to rest on my knee. "It'll be okay," Susan says, though I don't hear the honesty in her tone. I can see the healing burn marks on her fingertips and hear the slur of her words because of missing teeth, and I want to shout at her that it won't be. "We get fed, and most of the time, we're left alone."

I drop my hands to my thighs and turn to glare at her. "Nothing about this is going to be okay. Nothing, Susan."

She gives me a sympathetic look, one that tells me everything she isn't saying: I have no choice but to endure what comes next.

Fresh tears prick and spill down my cheeks. Children terrify me. Being taken against my will terrifies me. Never being found again terrifies me. And yet, there's absolutely nothing I can do. My choices had been stripped of me the moment I was thrown into the van. *No.* The moment I received the lily, the moment I knew I was being hunted like a deer in Open Season.

"Oh, god," I sob.

She squeezes my knee, and it does nothing to comfort me. I cry for a while, letting the tears flow because everything – my entire life – is now over, and everything from here on out won't be my choice. I'll be violated in the most unspeakable ways, and the thought makes me gag a few times.

When my cheeks are raw and my eyes are puffy, I peer at my palms as I ask Susan, "How long have they been here?"

She blows out a breath and glances at the other two. It's then that I notice the brand on her wrist. "They came from Vermont with *him* and his kids. There used to be three but one . . ." she trails off and glances at me knowingly.

"Died," I murmur.

"Yeah," she sighs out. Her lips twitch like she doesn't want to say what she plans to next, but then she blurts quietly, "He usually only ever has three women. Or so they told me when you got dragged down here. I was to replace the third. But you?"

I wipe my cheeks and turn a frown to her. "Why me?"

"I don't know," she breathes so quietly that I almost didn't hear it. "Did you do something to earn his attention?"

I shake my head. "I don't even know what he looks like."

She opens her mouth to say something, but a door opens and floods a light on the stairs I hadn't seen until now. Footsteps follow until they come into sight clad in men's tennis shoes, then a pair of legs, then a torso with a plaid button-up. Another set of adult feet follows behind the first man.

When the first man comes into view, all the air is sucked from my lungs. He strides right for me with those puppy dog eyes, the ones I thought were harmless. The ones I didn't know belonged to a predator.

"Hi, Tori," Josiah says clear as day, breaking through what was once a quiet, dooming conversation. It's almost too loud for my ears, too loud for the space.

The women on the other wall cower, but Susan remains strong by my side, squeezing my thigh to keep me in reality when all I want to do is pretend that none of this exists.

"I don't understand," I say, my throat clogged with disbelief that someone I'd grown to care about is right before me, bending at the knees to be eye level with me.

I look behind him to find the second man standing somewhat in the shadows. Even though it's darker where he hovers, I can see the scars across his face. Fresh scars that are still puffy, and I know then and there that this is the man that Killian tortured. It has to be.

I can see Josiah in him. They have the same curly hair and the same thickness. Their eyes are different though. Where Josiah's is calm and collected, this man's eyes are wild. Unsure.

In his arms, he holds a toddler. The toddler, with curly hair and pudgy cheeks, watches on silently.

He reaches and taps my chin, and I veer away in disgust. "Ask your questions, and I'll give you answers."

"So freely?" I hiss.

He shrugs. "It's not like you have anyone to tell. Besides, I keep my girls informed."

Realization dawns on me. His big family. His father I've never seen – the guy Killian tortured who knew that he was working with someone. "You're him," I gasp. "You're the Lillian. These are your kids." I point to the ceiling in emphasis then look past him to the toddler who watches me.

His smile pulls me back to him. It's sweet, nothing telling to the snake behind it. "You came to that conclusion faster than I thought you would. Killian must have been telling you stories."

I narrow my eyes at him. "That's why you don't like Killian, isn't it? You knew who he was, what he'd done to your father." I took a guess that the man behind him was his dad, but by the way his smile twitches, I know that I'm right. "You killed his family!"

"My father is a good man. He didn't deserve what Killian did to him. What kind of son would I be if he didn't pay for his actions?"

I laugh without humor. "Your father is a man who kidnaps helpless women so that his son can rape them and build the perfect family."

Josiah shrugs again. "None of those things are wrong, but you make it sound so dirty."

"That's because it is," I spit. "Is that what you plan to do with me, Josiah? Hmm? Force yourself on me and make me carry your baby?"

He reaches to touch my face again, but this time, I move before the contact. "You're the most impure woman I've met who's absolutely captured my attention. But I can change that for you, your purity. In the eyes of God, you'll be pure again once we're united."

"You mean once you've raped me. Doesn't sound so damn pure now, does it?"

"You're upset," he observes out loud.

"Damn right I am. Let me go!"

"That'd be a shame to do since Pastor Kent went through all that trouble to help me get you here."

A tear forces its way out my right eye and trails a hot path down to my mouth where I taste the salt. "He's a bastard. You're all bastards!"

"Now, that's not fair. Just because he doesn't like you, it doesn't mean he doesn't want to save you."

I snarl at him. "What a coincidence that two creeps met each other in such a small town."

"Oh no," he begins with a shake of his head. "We didn't meet here. We met in New York when my father and I visited his church. We moved out here shortly after him, a few weeks ago."

"What? You mean when you chased that woman trying to escape? The woman I killed? Were you what? Moving them?"

He nods with surprised eyes. "That was my father, but I didn't know it was you who killed her at the time. She was my favorite you know… until you came along. I'm sure you'll make just as pretty babies."

"You are fucking sick." I spit in his face.

He doesn't move to wipe it away. "Did you at least like my lily?"

I lean to spit on his face again, but he moves out of the way just in time for it to sail over his shoulder. "Was that you or Kent?"

He waves a hand around the space between us dismissively, and as he finally wipes my spit from his cheek and sticks it in his mouth to suckle on, he eventually says, "Pastor Kent doesn't do my dirty work, Tori. He just helps me move the women since my father can't do it anymore. Not with a face like his, not after what your little boyfriend did to him."

I rake my hands down my face, wiping my eyes while disbelieving but knowing everything he said isn't a lie. "You were in my house." I don't know what's worse – him or Kent.

"I was. Even though I wanted to snoop, I didn't stay long. I thought you might appreciate that." He stands up and heads to the wall with no women chained to it against their will. A shelf stands there meant for canned goods, and on the shelf are things I cannot identify.

"What are you doing?" I demand with a shaky voice. I look to the father, but he just watches on with those same manic eyes. "Please. Please make him let me go."

"He won't listen to you," Josiah says with his back still turned toward me. "My father loves me. He gives me what I want most. He knows my work is for our Lord, and he plans to stay the course."

"What now?" I shout. "Hmm? What happens now?"

He turns back toward me, and through the light of the upstairs, I see a syringe in his hand. He heads back toward me. "Now, I brand you, but I assume you don't want to be awake for me to mark you as mine."

"Fuck. Off," I bite out as I scramble further backward. My spine hits the wall at the same time he reaches me. I grab onto Susan's arm and start to beg her. "Please! Please don't let him do this to me!"

"I'm sorry, Tori," she sobs out. "I can't–"

"Please!"

"While you're out," he says above my pleas, "I'll check to see where you're at in your cycle. If you're ovulating, we'll begin."

"Please! Please, Susan!"

And then he grabs my hair roughly, yanks my head to the side, and jabs the needle into my neck.

Chapter 31

Kilian Savage

I BARGE into Pierce's police station, and luck must be on my side because he's actually in there instead of patrolling the town. He looks ready though, leaning against the front desk as though he'd been waiting for someone to arrive. Me?

Behind him is the last person I least expected, but it only confirms that I'm the one Pierce is waiting on. Why else would Cole be here? Is he here to protect Pierce against me? Is he here because he's thick as thieves with Derek? Either way, I'm immediately on the defensive.

Cole stands there with his arms crossed, his expression pinched and stressed. Paint covers his jeans, and his cut-off shows his bunched-up biceps, coiled tightly like the wrinkle lines between his brows.

I don't know what look is on my face, but Pierce and Cole meet me halfway, and immediately, Pierce opens his mouth. "Tegan called when you left the store."

With zero fucks to give right now, I ask, "Did you ever

even get the warrant for your grandfather?" I'm ready to play the blame game because, in my opinion, he is to blame.

He narrows his eyes at me. "I know you're scared, but you don't need to take it out on me."

"The fuck I don't." I ball my fingers into fists and step into his space. "This could have been prevented if you'd just done your job."

"Killian," Cole murmurs. He comes to stand by both our sides and uses his hands to push us a few more inches apart. "This isn't going to solve anything."

I ignore him and continue to direct my questions at Pierce. "Answer me."

Pierce sighs and pinches the bridge of his nose. With closed eyes, he says, "I didn't need to. He let me and the guys search his place without one. We found nothing but a few lilies he took from the field." He drops his hand back to his side and looks me square in the eye. "Everyone takes flowers from that field. It wasn't enough to take him in aside from vandalizing."

"When did you search his place?" Cole asks. He crosses his arms, and if I didn't know any better, I'd say he was on my side. I look at him for a moment, a little surprised, before I turn my attention back to the sheriff.

"A few hours ago," he answers, looking slightly guilty but still holding his ground with me.

"Before or after he took Tori?" Cole interjects for me. All I want to do is strangle this man with nothing but a noose, and Cole must know that.

He scrubs the back of his head. "Based on the time stamp of the video Tegan sent me, it was before."

Through a clamped jaw, I ask, "Where is he now?"

He looks down the hall. "I had a bad feeling and took him in for vandalizing about an hour ago. And then I saw the camera feed… Look, he doesn't know that Tori had cameras, nor the true reason I now hold him." He looks back at me. "I really didn't know he was involved in this. I really thought you guys were wrong, that I knew him well enough to believe he wasn't capable of this. I feel like I should apologize."

"You should," Cole grunts. "Because now Tegan's best friend is missing, and the only person who could possibly tell us where she is happens to be related to you, and you chose to ignore any and all signs."

Pierce looks down at his shoes and stuffs his hands into his uniform's pockets. "I care about Tori too, you know."

"Apparently, not enough," I growl. This asshole gets no claim to her. He lost that right the moment he chose to ignore her first inkling about who was the dangerous one. He deserves nothing, not even sympathy. There's a special place in hell for people like him because, in my opinion, he's just as guilty as his grandfather.

His nostrils flare as he exhales. "I can't let you into the interrogation room."

"Why?" I demand. I know I could get the answers a lot faster than he could.

"Because we have to do this with the law on our side, Savage. Letting someone like you interrogate him for answers will only raise more questions than actual convictions. Even I can't interrogate him. One of the other guys is leading it, and we have someone else going through his phone."

I flex my jaw and look away. I want nothing more than to make Kent hurt for what he's done. Demand answers one broken bone at a time.

"He's right, Killian," Cole mutters. "And you know it."

I look at Cole. "Would you be okay with sitting by if this were Tegan?"

His lips twitch with distaste for whatever feeling that brought about inside him, but he answers, "No, but I'd also know that, if I messed any of this up by not listening, I'd never forgive myself."

I huff, even though he's making complete sense.

Satisfied that he got through to me, he turns to Pierce. "Hurry up."

Pierce nods, and with one last glance at me, he takes off down the hall and eventually disappears into a room. The sudden silence besides my heavy breathing engulfs me, threatening to choke me. I start to pace as Cole stands there and watches me. Doing nothing is not in my nature. I'm a man of action, a man who gets answers no matter the cost, and here I am, not allowed to do anything.

"You know," Cole begins. "We don't know each other, we don't even know anything about each other, but something similar happened with Tegan last year."

Without looking at him, I turn and make another stride in the opposite direction. "Did Tegan get taken for the purpose of being bred like some bitch dog?"

Silence. Utter silence aside from my shoes tapping on the tile. "No," he eventually says. "But it was just as devastating."

"What are you trying to tell me?" I ask, whipping to face him because I cannot stand the inner turmoil. His wife turned out fine. My girl won't be, even if she survives. Even if we find her, we could be too late. She could have irreversible damage that I can't call her back from. I'll lose her in a different way than I lost my wife, and I don't know what's worse: death or *this.*

"I don't know," Cole says, swiping a hand down his face. "Faith, maybe."

Faith. After everything I've done, everything I've witnessed, having faith for something that's in the hands of the human race isn't one of them.

"Why are you even here?" I rumble low and dangerously. I know he hasn't done anything wrong, but Pierce is no longer here, and I need someone to point my anger at.

Thankfully, he doesn't take offense to my hostility. He takes a seat on the front of the desk and looks at me tiredly.

"To support Tegan. To make sure Tori is found. You're not the only one who cares about her, you know."

"You don't know anything," I hiss. "You don't even know a single thing about me. About me and her, even. You know *nothing*." I spit the last word.

I have to give him credit; he doesn't rise to my tone, even though every ounce of me wants him to. "I don't need to. You love her, it's as simple as that."

My head whips back as if I'd been popped in the mouth, and I blink at him. "What?" I ask because his words filtered in my head, but they didn't settle there.

He shrugs one shoulder as if it's not a big deal. "Everyone who has been watching you knows you love her." He raises an eyebrow at me. "I'm surprised you don't."

"You don't know what you're talking about."

"I do, actually." He smirks, and all I want to do is wipe it from his face. "Go ahead. Tell me it's not true."

Because I can't growl out those words, I start pacing again. I love my wife. I want her and my family's revenge, but it's no longer about *just* that. The moment I saw that camera feed, it became something else. It was devastating and destructive to my soul to know that I may never see Tori again, that the Lillian might win all over again but in a whole different way. The thought of losing Tori makes me want to stop breathing, to stop existing because, not only is this my fault but . . .

I love her.

The thought hits me like a train, and I take a step back as if I'd almost been struck by one.

"And there it is," Cole murmurs.

My face hardens because now, with the realization that my confusing feelings were actually that of love, I'll stop at nothing to get her back, even if she doesn't come back to me whole.

"I'm going to kill him."

"I know," Cole says straight-faced. As if he's privy to the

knowledge of the Lillian. About my family. As if he knew I wasn't talking about the pastor. "But," he adds softly. "Speaking from experience, rotting in jail is far worse than death."

I narrow my eyes at him. "You seriously want me to go by the law here? Would you?"

He shakes his head. "No. I'd make him pay and then kill him slowly. But this isn't me, and since I'm the one with a level head, I'm qualified for the advice. Let the law handle this, Killian."

"I don't know if I can," I admit.

He scratches the side of his head and sighs. "I once got advice from Tori, and I'm going to give you the same advice: Don't murder him and then end up in jail yourself. Think of what that would do to Tori if we ever get her back."

I want nothing more than to snarl for throwing Tori's words at me, words that were never said to me, advice that she had never given me. But I know she would now. She would say the same thing, and even though she doesn't like Pierce, she'd tell me to stay on the side of the law.

The door opens, and Pierce strides down the hall. His face is as red as a tomato, and I know whatever happened in there pissed him off. *Good.*

Another cop I recognize from the search at Tori's house follows closely behind him, and when Pierce reaches us, he dismisses him. Once he's gone, he says to us, "He refused to talk and asked for a lawyer, but they found something on his phone - numerous calls to and from one number."

"Who?" I demand.

He looks me square in the eyes. "What do you know about Tori's employee, Josiah Cruise?"

Chapter 32

Tori Townsend

MY HEAD POUNDS when I come back to consciousness. It thuds at the same beat as my heart, right in the center of my temples. Being drugged twice in less than twenty-four hours will do that, and it definitely can't be good for my health.

A bright light shines against my closed eyelids, and my eyes begin to water because of it, enough so that the tears are seeping through. The salty droplets slide down my cheekbones and gather in the hollow of my ears because whatever I'm lying on has me on my back.

I move to wipe the next tear away, only to find that my hand – both of them – are tied down. My eyes fly open, and I immediately move to sit up, but my middle is strapped to a slightly padded exam table.

My breathing picks up a pace, and I peer down the old dress I'm wearing – a dress similar to the woman I hit – and down further to my bare legs that are strapped far apart from one another in stirrups.

Breath captures in my lungs when I come to the realization that he dressed me. While I was out, he stripped me bare and dressed me…

I start to hyperventilate, exposed and vulnerable to this cold room. The chill wraps around my bare sex left open for view to whoever walks into the room.

The room is definitely part of the basement as it has the same walls and the same musty smell. To the left is a metal, rusted cabinet that you'd see in a medical clinic, and to the right is a metal tray on wheels. From the angle I'm at, I can't see what's on the tray, but whatever is there has fear creeping down my spine in cold and thin tendrils.

There are no windows here, nothing to tell how much time has passed since I was knocked out. It could have been a full day for all I know, and somehow, that leaves me with a guttural pit in the bottom of my stomach. If I was going to be saved, I would have been by now. It's not like those who'd save me would have far to go, and if they're not here, it's not going to happen.

They have no idea where I am.

The only thing lighting the space is the large circular lamp that's shining over my body, making my exposed skin glow. A slight ache draws me to my wrist, and I clench and unclench my fingers to relieve the burning ache, but it only makes it worse.

The ache is right where the brand was on the woman, so I can only imagine that Josiah made good on his promise to brand me as his with a lily tattoo of my own. Even if I ever get out of this, even if I'm rescued, it will always be a reminder of what I'm about to endure because the only reason that I'm strapped to a table, left exposed to the room, is because he found out that I'm in my prime time to be impregnated.

I start to gag at that thought. Gag for fear. Gag for revolution. Gag because the spike of anxiety is so great that my body repells it the only way it knows how.

I tip my head to the side, and vomit spurts from my mouth and splats on the concrete ground. I heave until what little was in my stomach is gone, and then I heave some more until little specks of black flood my vision. When it finally subsides, I scream and fight against my restraints, but it's no use. I'm not going anywhere. Completely helpless is exactly what I am.

As an answer to my scream, I hear heavy footsteps outside my room's door. The urge to gag comes again when it's opened and Josiah's head pops through the opened crack. The first thing he does is glance at me, and then he slides his gaze to my exposed pussy. A hunger lights his eyes, and tears prick my own because I know, no matter what, I'm going to be fucked against my will.

He steps inside and shuts the door softly behind him as if my cries of frustration don't still echo around the room. "No need to get upset, Tori," he says calmly.

"Fuck you," I whimper.

The clucking of his tongue, as he travels over to my knees, makes my hair stand on end. I'm keenly aware of his nearness, and I tip my head to the side so that I don't have to see whatever he plans to do down there.

Something touches my pussy – a finger, I realize – and it slides from the mound all the way down and circles my entrance. I try to slide away, but the straps around my middle keep me exactly where he wants me.

"You're ovulating, you know," he whispers with so much heat and intention that I close my eyes tightly shut.

"Please don't touch me," I beg in a whimper. "Just let me go."

"I can't do that," he answers back in a clear, hurtful tone. He inserts a finger inside me, and I clench my teeth together so tight that my jaw aches. I try desperately to think of something else, anything else, besides what he's doing. "So ready for a baby, aren't you? For my baby. You're mine now, Tori. And soon, you'll realize that."

"Stop," I beg. "Please stop."

"You may not be ready for me yet," he begins, taking his finger out of me. "But you will be. Soon, maybe after we've had our first child together, you'll beg for another."

I snap my gaze to him, and even through my watery eyes, I narrow them dangerously at him. "I will never beg for anything from you, you sick and twisted fuck."

A smile grows on his face. "So much spirit." He pats my knee. "That'll fade with time."

"I'll never be okay with you screwing me, Josiah," I say angrily. "I'll never be okay with carrying your child. I'll never be okay even in your presence."

The smile starts to fade from his face. "Perhaps we will do as my father suggests this time."

"What?" I ask.

He travels to the cabinet, and I follow him with my eyes. I have no idea what's in there, and I am not sure I want to find out. Not that I could see what's inside. The lamp over my body is pretty blinding to the rest of the things around me.

"My father was an OBGYN," he begins as he opens it. The hinges squeal, and he starts digging around inside, picking up things and examining them as if they have answers to some sort of question in his head. "There are other methods to get you pregnant that we could try. That he suggested, anyway."

"What? Does he not like you raping anyone?"

He glances back at me, but there are too many shadows to make out his expression. "Honestly," he mutters, and the way he says it makes him sound as youthful as he's supposed to be. "I don't think he likes any of this. But he loves me, and since my mother died and I'm the only one left – me and my children – he'd do anything for us. Keeping the secret of who I am. Of what I do. Of what I need. My desires and wishes. He gives me the world so that I can have it all."

"You're fucking sick."

"I'm just doing God's work," he claims as he turns back to the cabinet.

"So? What? You're not going to rape me?"

"Rape is such a harsh word," he says as he grabs something, and then he unzips his jeans. The sound of his zipper is daunting, and for a second, my mind forces me to envision what his huffing and puffing over me, pushing in and out of me, will feel like, both physically and mentally.

"It's the correct word." My voice cracked several times throughout that sentence.

With his pants hanging slightly off him, he heads back to me. He has a small, clear cup in his hand, and he pulls the table over to my hips and sets it on top of it.

"What are you doing?" I demand, my expression wild as he pushes down his pants and underwear to the middle of his thighs. His cock springs free, and I start to cry. An ugly cry, a fearful cry, a cry of such emotional pain that it threatens to drown me.

He shushes me in a loving manner. "I won't take you today. I'll do as my father suggested, and he'll implant you with my seed. If that doesn't work, however . . ."

Hope fills me, and for a second, I hiccup my next sobs. I don't want to be pregnant, but I'd rather be pregnant by insemination than actual, physical rape.

I witness him grab his cock and start to pump as he watches my pussy, and then I look away. I can't. The noises he begins to make are enough to make me want to gouge sharpened pencils into my eardrums. And when he touches me again, I squeeze my eyes shut.

I can hear his hand pumping up and down his cock, feel his finger probe my sex, and fresh flowing tears spill down my cheeks in endless ribbons. Time seems to go by slowly as he grunts and groans and slides his finger up and down over my sex to get himself off.

I don't know how it's come to this and how my life has

become this. I don't know what I did to end up in this situation, what sort of god I pissed off to get me here. But I do know one thing: I don't deserve this. No one does.

His moan is long and low, and by the sound of his slowing, pumping hand, I know he's getting ready to cum. And with it, with that climax, my fate is sealed.

Chapter 33

Killian Savage

PIERCE'S SHERIFF'S car skids to a halt outside that kid's home, and I grip the dashboard on the passenger side to keep from putting my forehead through the glass due to the force of the stop. No sirens. No flashing cherries. The last thing we want is attention drawn to us.

Josiah Cruise. I saw his picture. I saw his social media, his known addresses, his love life, which doesn't and didn't exist. Tegan told us all she knew about him too. How he had a thing for Tori, how they thought it was innocent. She blames herself, which she shouldn't. He doesn't look like he'd do anything like this. He looks like a simple kid. A young man who received the highest honors in high school back on the coast. A nerd maybe, but a breeder? And for this long?

This had to have begun when he went through puberty. When he could actually conceive a child, and right around that time, the first woman was taken, and his father disappeared from his practice.

It makes me sick that this could happen. This child

conceived children while he was in high school against the women's will. And the worst part? No one knew. No one had a clue. Those of us who knew something was going on blamed the father. We never thought of looking for a son. What kind of person would allow his son to become this?

A weak-minded man.

Regret fills me because I should have tortured the father further. I should have tried harder to get answers back in New York because, if I had, this never would have happened. They never would have fled to Fairview, and Tori never would have been taken. But there is no greater service than a man protecting his child. I just wish I had had that same opportunity.

The whole way here, I hoped that we wouldn't be too late because, the whole time we were researching the kid, I couldn't help but think of our time together and how, not once had she had her period. I've had kids and a good woman. I know a woman's cycle, and Tori had to be close to her ovulation.

I clench my teeth because, even though she hasn't been with Josiah for a full day, he could have already bred her. *Bred.* Raped is more like it, and that thought alone makes me want to punch the man next to me.

Instead of doing just that, I grab the door handle and kick it open with more force than necessary. I'm going to get my girl back. I'm going to save her, and then …

Cole's words filter through my head, the ones about murder, about going to jail for it, and how that would affect Tori. Even though I want to kill them both, I can't do that to Tori because, after thinking of the worst of the worst, I realized one thing: I love her more than I thought I did. It had all snapped into place the longer Cole's observation settled. All those confusing feelings and emotions had perfectly assembled until all that was there was this dire need to never let her go. To get her back and never let her out of my sight. My heart had beat faster, and my skin had covered in a slick sweat when the realization struck – by the time I get to her, she could be a completely different Tori, and the last thing she'd want to hear is that I love her.

So, instead of going in there myself, snapping their necks, and grabbing my girl, I'm going to do this by the law. She'd want that, no matter the state she's in. I know what it's like to lose the people you love, and I won't give the universe an excuse for Tori to endure it even if she ends up not wanting me.

Pierce hops out of his car as two other cop cars squeal up to the property. I slam the door at the same time Pierce does and get a good look at the four walls that house hell. It's a simple farmhouse, white with a rock garden. Two stories high. Sheds dot the small acreage, and a small barn sits off to the left. Even though it's twilight, chickens roam about and peck along the ground, and inside the house, filtering out to us is the sound of a crying child.

The sound grates on my nerves because I know exactly how that child was conceived. And I know that somewhere in that house, women are being held, one of them *mine.*

The other cops climb out of their cars just as fast as we did. Their guns are out of their holsters immediately as they head in our direction.

"How are we doing this?" I ask because I have plenty of ways that I want to do this.

Pierce pulls out his gun and turns to face me. Over the roof of the car, he says, "You're going to stay here."

"The fuck I am," I growl as I thump my fist on the roof.

"Killian!" he says. His using my first name since the first time we met is enough to give me pause. "You're too close to this!"

The child crying in the house immediately stops at Pierce's shout, and we all freeze and glance toward the house. Through one of the windows, a man stands. A man I recognize. His face is scarred to hell from what I did to him, but I'd know him anywhere.

His expression is one of shock, and the next second later, he disappears back into the depths of the home.

"Move!" Pierce shouts to the other cops, and they begin rushing toward the house. "Stay," he adds to me with a point of his finger toward the ground.

I growl, and every muscle coils. And then Pierce is gone, leaving me fucking alone outside.

It takes me all of three seconds to spit, "fuck that," and race toward the house. Over my dead body will I not see Tori for myself. I can't leave it in the hands of people I don't know nor trust because, for all we know, the bastards will kill everyone inside before they allow us to arrest them.

As soon as I get inside and reach the living room, I find the father pressed up against the far wall by Pierce. He's cuffing him, reading him his rights, while the children around us sob with wide eyes and fingers in their mouths. One cop is trying to move them to the other side of the living room, but all they want to do is watch on as their grandfather is arrested.

The kids range from at least four years old to the toddler in the playpen. There are four of them, and it's enough to give me pause. The breath rushes out of me as adrenaline courses through my veins. In seemingly slow motion, I turn back toward Pierce and the scar-faced bastard.

My feet move before I instruct them to, and before I know it, I have the father's collar in my fist and my face inches from his. "Did you kill my family?" I promised them revenge, and even though I can't directly give it to them, I can put a face to their death.

The father's eyes are wild as he searches my face. Even though I wore a mask to each and every job, I know he knows me. I can tell by his wide expression, by the stench of fear that causes perspiration at his temples.

Pierce looks back and forth between us but keeps him pressed against the wall.

I grit my teeth and spit out, "Did you kill my family?"

The father begins to stutter, and I look on as Pierce grabs his back and shoves him harder into the wall. "Answer him!" he demands. "Or I swear to god, I will make your life a living hell even while you rot in jail."

I blink, surprised that Pierce is backing me up, but recover quickly by gripping the father's jaw and forcing him to look at me once more. "What he'll do to you is child's play," I rumble dangerously. "Try another night with me."

What I said must be enough because I hear a little whimper starting at the back of his throat. It's almost as satisfying as the cries I had planned to yank out of him back when this was just about my family's revenge.

With his face all smooshed in my grip, he utters, "No," to me.

I roughly let him go because I had a feeling that one man couldn't pull off my entire family's murder. Not this fool, not by himself.

As Pierce yanks him from the wall and passes him to a cop, I start stomping through the house. "Savage!" he hisses after me.

I don't listen. I keep marching through the short hallway until I reach the kitchen. I have every intention of finding his bastard son. All I can see is red. All I hear is the blood rushing through my ears. All I feel is every nerve lit on fire.

Pierce grabs my arm and comes to stand before me. I hadn't realized I'd been heaving for air until he presses a palm to my chest. "Calm down."

"Get out of my way."

"You don't even know where you're going. We haven't found the son, the women, or Tori yet."

"You searched the house?"

"One of my men did, yes." He removes his hand and rubs the back of his neck.

"The upstairs and this floor?"

His eyebrows raise at my condescending tone, but he gives me a curt nod.

"And the basement?"

By his expression, he hadn't thought of the basement. I growl under my breath as I stomp through the kitchen and head toward the dining room. I hadn't seen a single basement entrance in my short time here, and the only place left that I haven't searched is the dining room.

Highchairs and booster seats are tucked in a corner, and I kick them aside as I thunder by, Pierce close on my heels. I find a door here, right in the middle of the dining room wall, and I know without a doubt that it leads to a basement.

I don't wait for Pierce's instruction before I open the door. I'm greeted with a set of steep stairs that disappear into darkness. The stench of a normal, damp basement stuffs its way up my nose, and it only fuels me to begin taking the stairs two at a time.

As soon as I reach the bottom and my eyes adjust, I stop and get a good look at what I just walked into.

"My god," Pierce whispers behind me.

I swallow thickly because, even though it's dark, along one wall are two very pregnant women. They're dirty and covered in an even dirtier blanket. Chains are attached to the wall, and their length disappears under the blanket.

"The police," a woman's voice says across from me. I swivel my gaze and squint into the deep shadow that is that space. A woman sits there – same chains, same blanket as the others – but if she's pregnant, she's not showing yet.

Pierce steps around me and heads to the pregnant women first. "Who has the key," he says softly to them while he tugs on one of their chains.

I look straight at the woman across from me because I'm

no fool. Next to her is a chain with no one on the end. An empty spot. *Tori's spot.*

I step farther into the basement, clenching and unclenching my fist to keep my fear at bay. "Where's Tori? Where's the Lillian?" Because I know wherever they are, they're together, and god knows what hell is going on, and only angels know what she's enduring.

The woman lifts her arm and points to another section of the basement. A door stands there that I hadn't seen until this very moment. Like where she sits, it's in a dark pocket of the basement.

I immediately head to it, and lifting my foot, I kick it open.

Chapter 34

Tori Townsend

THE DOOR SHATTERS as it's kicked in, and the wood shards bounce off the wall and clatter to the ground. My eyes are wild as I take in the silhouette of Killian's coiled frame, my neck craned so that the scalpel that's pressed to my artery doesn't knick the skin.

I'm still strapped to the table, still exposed, but instead of standing between my thighs, Josiah is behind me, threatening my very life if Killian takes one step closer.

His hand doesn't shake. His hand is poised, confident, as if he fully plans to take my life, no matter what, and that thought alone causes my hands to tremble. I squeeze them into fists in hopes that it doesn't shake my whole body because, if it does, I'll seal my own fate.

We had heard the commotion outside, someone shouting, and then heard the stomping upstairs as people entered. The crying of children, more shouts. It hadn't taken long for Josiah to realize we'd been found, and he had headed to the cabinet, grabbed the first sharp object he found, and waltzed right back to me. *Waltzed.* Some may even say it was a swagger.

I wish I had seen it before, the crazy inside him. I never would have hired him, but I've quickly learned that he had been fixated on me the moment he applied. Maybe before then. He would have taken me even if he wasn't my employee. There was nothing I could have done differently but simply not exist at all.

They stand there like that, Killian making choices in his head while Josiah waits for him to choose. I can't make out Killian's face with the light still shining and half-blinding me. If I can't see his face, then neither can Josiah, and for some odd reason, that gives me a little comfort. He can't see the calculations that are surely going on in Killian's head. He can't read him.

"You have two choices," Josiah murmurs to Killian. "You can turn around and walk out, leaving me with my girl to walk off into the sunset with, or you can try to kill me."

Killian says nothing, and I whimper once more as the skin splits with the tighter hold Josiah has on the scalpel.

"If you try to kill me," he continues, "I'll take her first, and then you truly will have no one, Killian Savage."

A fine sweat breaks across my spine, pricking the pores and causing me to force down a shiver. I can see the shadow of Killian's fingers curling into his palms as he makes his decision. Part of me fears that he just might walk away, so I whisper, "I'd rather be dead than go anywhere with you, you sick fuck."

Killian takes a threatening step inside the room when Josiah chuckles darkly. It's then that I can make out his face because the light hits it just right. His expression is hard, his lips set in a thin line and his eyes narrowed to slits and fixated on the man, the man-child, behind me.

Slowly, Killian's eyes slide down Josiah's poised arm to the scalpel at my neck and the bead of blood that drips down the slope. And then his eyes meet mine. Together, we hold a silent exchange, a conversation that needs no words at all. He'd rather I be dead too than go through any more of the pain that Josiah has to offer. Because that's what I'd live – a life of emotional damage, an existence of eternal misery. It wouldn't even be a life. I'd be a prisoner, an incubator, until one day, it would kill me. Whether that death would be by my own hand, fate's, or Josiah's, it doesn't matter.

Even though his eyes are set into slits displaying his rage, I can see the sorrow there. The pain. It's then I know that he feels something for me, that the very thought of me being gone may just do him in. It does little to comfort me, not in this moment. But we don't have a choice now, do we?

Killian's eyes flick to Josiah's, and I start to tremble, awaiting my own death. "Did you do it?"

I can hear the smile in his voice when he asks, "Do what?" All three of us know, by that tone alone, that Josiah knows exactly what he's talking about.

Killian's asking if he did the job. If he raped me.

"Did you force yourself on her?" Killian rumbles in such a dark and dangerous way that even my own body wants to recoil.

"I guess, if she survives, you'll find out in nine months."

Killian's jaw ripples as he flexes it, and I can see him weigh just exactly how he's going to make him pay. He looks at me once more and I watch as tears gather in his angry eyes. "I love you, Tori," he whispers. "And I'm sorry."

I don't have time to revel in the idea that he feels the same way for me. To wish I had one more second to tell him the same words. To think of what we are to each other and dream of what we could be. I don't even have time to tense as he thunders forward. Instead, I close my eyes, waiting for the sharp pain and the warm blood as my life slips away from me.

A single tear slips out of my squeezed eyes, and just as I suck in a breath, a boom rocks the room, and a thud quickly follows. The breath whooshes out of me, and my eyes fly open. Ears ringing, I glance beside the table to where Killian is staring at something on the floor. It's then I realize that the scalpel is no longer at my neck and the insane man is no longer standing behind me. I don't feel the sickening heat from his body nor smell the stench of his sweat from getting himself off. Instead, cold air swirls around my scalp.

Something steps out of the shadows of the door, and my attention quickly moves to it. Pierce comes into the light, his gun pointed at where Josiah had just been standing, and my heart skips a wild beat. *The boom was a gunshot.*

For a moment, the three of us remain there in silence, Killian's chest heaving while he stares at what surely is Josiah's body, Pierce, calm and collected, positioned to take another shot, and me, shaking so bad that the exam bed I'm on rattles. And then Killian peels his gaze away from the man who took his family from him, the man who about took me too, and turns his attention to me. His eyes zoom in on my neck, but I can feel that the knick there isn't life-threatening. I only feel tiny beads of blood that have already cooled against my skin.

"Is he-" I swallow thickly. "Is he dead?"

My hollow voice is enough to stir him into action. He heads to me and begins to untie my legs first, and once they're free and I'm no longer exposed to the room, he gently pulls down my dress to cover my sex. Without saying anything, he frees the rest of me and helps me sit up. Once I am, he takes my face in his hands and presses his lips so hard to mine that I'm sure he'll leave a bruise.

When we both need air, he pulls away and rests his forehead against mine. His chest still heaves from adrenaline, and my body still trembles with fear, but we wait there for a moment, sharing space we both thought we'd never have again.

A sob racks my chest as Pierce crosses the room and bends to where Josiah's body lies. Because he didn't fire his gun again, I know that he's dead. It's over. But as my body continues to tremble, I ask myself, is it really?

Killian gathers me into his arms, wraps my legs around him, and picks me up. I hold on tight and sob against his shoulder. The tears flow freely, and try as I might, I can't stop them. I can't control the quaking of my body. I can't take away the memories that flood my mind.

With one hand holding me up around the waist, he tangles his fingers in my hair, tucks his face in the crook of my neck, and inhales deeply. "It's over," he murmurs against my skin. I hear more emotion in his voice than I've ever heard, and it only serves to make me cry harder. "It's over, dollface. It's over."

"I-I-I can't – breathe," I choke out.

"Get her out of here," I hear Pierce say, and Killian doesn't need more instruction. He takes me from the room in long strides, climbs the stairs with me still in his arms as if I weigh nothing at all, and the next thing I know, we're in the warmer climate of the outdoors. Of freedom. It's something I thought I'd never have again.

I suck in precious evening air as I'm set on the trunk of a cop car, and Killian pulls his chest away from me to grip both sides of my face. He looks at me, takes in my wild expression, and whispers to me, "Breathe. Take a deep breath."

Even though it's difficult, I do as he instructs.

"Another," he commands softly.

We repeat this until my breathing is more hiccups than hyperventilation, and once I've calmed enough, he pushes hair from my sweaty face and gently presses his lips to my forehead. He lingers there for a moment, and when he pulls away, I can see all the pain on his face.

"He-He was going to make me carry his b-baby."

"I know," he responds hoarsely, petting my hair once more. "Did he-"

He leaves the sentence lingering there, but I know exactly

what he's asking. I give a shake to my head. "He didn't rape me." I see his shoulders relax slightly, and I angrily wipe away some of the tears at the edge of my jaw. "He was going to do some sort of medical procedure to make me pregnant."

I watch as Killian swallows thickly. For a second, his gaze flicks below, between us. "Did he?"

I shake my head. "He didn't get the chance. You guys came crashing in." It's then that I look around. Pierce is at the front door, his phone in his hand as he calls for an ambulance to take a dead body away. Two other cops are by another cop's car, one on his phone while the other watches over the children I had heard in the house.

The other three women are by the other cop car, and I can see the dead look in everyone's eyes. It doesn't settle well with me that another day would give me the same look, the same void of emotions.

In the back of one of the cars is Josiah's father. Even though I only saw him in darkness, I'd recognize those features anywhere. There's a craze in the set of his face as he struggles with the cuffs holding his hands behind him. Either he heard the gunshot – the death of his one and only child – or the very thought of jail is worse than his own death.

"He deserves everything that's coming to him," I say to no one in particular and then wipe more of my tears because, seeing him in cuffs, knowing his son is dead, makes a sense of calm wash over me, ridding my body of the rest of the quakes.

I turn back to Killian. He's watching me with a nervous sort of energy, probably wondering what sort of state I'm in. I'd be wondering the same thing if the roles were reversed.

Swallowing with difficulty, because I still have a lump in my throat, I grab his hand and twine my fingers with his. "You said something back there. Did you mean it?"

He squeezes my hand and nods. "I meant it."

"And you would have killed me to save me?"

His jaw flexes, but he nods again. "You mean everything

to me, Tori." He brings up his other hand and swipes away my next tear. "The thought – I couldn't – I would have rather been alone the rest of my life than watch you for another second, knowing you'd be raped the rest of your life, knowing you'd be dead inside. I knew you'd rather be dead than endure such a life, and I was willing to take you from mine to keep you safe."

And though those words aren't much, I know they're everything. Another tear falls, and this time, he kisses it away. "I love you too," I whisper, and I mean every damn word. And the best part? I'm not afraid of it.

Chapter 35

Killian Savage

AS SOON AS I pull up in Tori's new car, a truck pulls in after me. The truck's engine vibrates my space inside the car, and I huff a little. I had noticed that the truck had been following me for a few blocks, but I knew whose car it was just by the color alone.

I hop out of the car I just bought my girl, and as soon as I turn toward the truck, I'm greeted by a brilliant smile from Tegan, who's in the passenger seat. Cole, on the other hand, has a neutral expression. By the dark circles under his eyes, he looks exhausted, but I remember those days. Those days of worrying about what he'll be like as a father, about the new financial hurdles he'll have to jump and parenting rivers he'll have to cross, are clearly here. He'll get through it just like I did.

Shutting the car's door, I lean my side against the car's window and wait for them to exit their vehicle. It doesn't take long for them to reach me, but instead of giving them a formal greeting, I stare at the wooden canister in Tegan's arms. "What is that?" I ask right away.

Tegan and Cole look down into her arms as if they forgot they even had it. "That woman's ashes," Tegan answers. Her smile fades a little at the seriousness of what she holds. "Pierce asked me to give it to Tori."

I give one curt nod.

Cole looks toward Tori's house to see if he can spot the woman inside. If all is still as I left it, Tori is napping on the couch. She has no idea that I left to meet Derek to pick up this car and drop off his loaner. If she had, she would have called by now.

After all that had happened, Derek lent a helping hand and picked the car up for me in the bigger city. He didn't owe me anything, and truth be told, I'm the one who owes him an explanation for the shit storm I brought to his town, but he said nothing on the matter.

Everyone knows about what happened at the Lillian's farm a week ago. People gathered to take care of the women, make sure they were fed and clothed, and had help finding their loved ones back on the coast. The children, the ones they birthed, went with them. They went through an evaluation to see if they'd be fit to be mothers after all they'd been through, but they passed.

Susan, the woman who was taken from Mount Pleasant, received the most warmth at her return. After a quick test at the hospital, it was confirmed that she is pregnant by that fuck-wad, but she took the news surprisingly well. Pierce had taken her under his wing, making sure she's cared for. If you ask me, he directed his smitten behavior from Tori to her. I could see something forming there when we were all in the hospital, but I left well enough alone because there were worse match-ups.

Besides, Susan is going to need all the love and care the world has to offer. All those women are. My girl included.

"How is she doing?" Cole asks. They'd been keeping their visits short so as to not overwhelm Tori, but I can tell they're itching for things to return to normal. Tegan's been running the shop, and thanks to Kent getting arrested for his crimes and the community wanting to support Tori, the business has been doing better than it had been. Or so Tori has reported to me, thanks to Tegan's daily updates.

I look at the house with him. The world, my girl's world, is a whole lot better without those assholes in it. "She's sleeping better than the last time you asked. Today is the first day that I left her alone, and since I didn't get a call from her, I'm guessing she's either asleep or she's getting more used to being alone in the house."

I turn back to Cole and watch as his head bobs in a nod. Tegan's lips are twisted downward. I know that she doesn't like her friend's state of mind, but I also know that she knows it takes time to heal those sorts of wounds.

While we've been holed up in the house, I heard all about Tegan's incident last year. It's a miracle she's still sane after what she endured. It's also a miracle that Cole lets her out of his sight to go to work. I wonder if I'll ever get to that point, where I trust the people around us to do no harm to the woman I love.

Tegan huffs and passes me the urn. "Here," she whispers.

I scowl and take the urn into the crook of my arm. "Don't you want to come in?" I ask because the gravel is crunching underfoot as they're turning to leave.

Tegan shakes her head. "She needs you more than me right now. And with that?" She tips her head toward the urn. She gives another shake of her head. "I can't give her what she needs right now."

The front door opens, and a sleepy-looking Tori pops her head out. Her face is set into a scowl until she takes us in. Then a small smile shows, and it's the most real smile I've seen since the moment I brought her home from the hospital.

She steps out and loosely crosses her arms over her chest. "Hey," she calls to us.

Tegan smiles back at her and adds an extra chipperness to her tone when she responds, "We were just leaving."

"So soon?" she asks.

"Cole's taking me baby supplies shopping," she answers back, and I don't know if it's a lie or if it's the truth, but they head back to the truck and climb inside anyway. With one last wave, they pull out of the driveway and disappear down the road.

When I look at her, Tori is already on her way over to me. She's looking at the car with interest. "Did something happen to Derek's car?"

"No," I say, patting the roof of her new car gently. "This is yours."

She flicks her gaze to me, eyebrows raised. "Mine?"

I nod and test a smile because I honestly don't know how she's going to react. Someone like Tori likes to be independent, and she's had to be for most of her life, but she has me now. She does not realize that nothing she could say or do would make me not take care of her. We may never get married because it's what we both don't want, but I have every intention of staying with her for the rest of my life. My drifting days are over; I'm building roots. I'm not going anywhere.

Her eyes narrow and I brace myself for some attitude. "It looks brand new."

"That's because it is."

"How'd you afford it?"

I scratch the back of my neck, feeling a little guilty. "My past life paid well."

She takes a moment to consider me before blowing out a breath. "That explains everything."

My eyebrows raise. "What's that supposed to mean?"

She shrugs a little. "How you could afford to live on the road and all that. But those days are over, right?"

I can see the insecurity in her expression, hear it in her voice, so I head around the car and tuck her into the arm that's not holding the urn and rumble, "We've talked about this."

"I know," she whispers. "But say it again."

I chuckle a little. "I love you, and I'm not leaving."

Her shoulders sag in relief, and if that's what it takes to make her feel safe again, I'll tell her every hour, every day, for the rest of my life.

We stand there for a minute or two, her arms wrapped around my middle and her cheek on my chest, before she even notices the urn. She raises her head from my chest and pokes the urn. "What's that?"

"The woman," I mutter carefully.

"Oh," she says, eyes wide. When she breathes out, she adds, "That feels like a lifetime ago."

Pierce and his men were never able to find where she belonged, let alone her name. Josiah's father didn't know either, not that he'd tell us anything at this point. He's more crazy than he is sane, and I get the feeling he never asked who a woman was, never questioned his son when he wanted someone taken. Her identity will always remain a mystery, and I don't know if that's more damaging or freeing for Tori.

Either way, I ask, "What do you want to do with her ashes?"

She raises her gaze away from the urn and to me. Gently, she peels away from me and takes the urn into her hands. "I want to scatter them in the field."

My raised eyebrows are my only visual of the question I don't voice.

She shrugs a little. "She deserves peace, and since that's our peaceful place, I figured that'd she like that."

"Are you sure?" I ask because I don't see us ever not

visiting that field again even though it's near the place where she was held hostage. In fact, we were just there yesterday. We hadn't gotten out of the car, but we sat there for a while and talked. And when we ran out of things to talk about, we fucked in the seat. I was a little surprised by that, considering everything Tori has been through, but her sexual appetite never changed. In fact, her need to feel loved in that way has only increased. I plan to give it to her as much as she asks, never pushing it, never asking for anything in return.

In a small voice, she says, "She deserves to have people watch over her. What better people than us? And-And I thought we could bury the picture of your family there too. Put them to final rest."

I swallow thickly at the emotion in her tone, at the conviction to see after a woman she killed, and at the loving way she wants to put my family at peace. It may have been an accident, and my family may have been out of her control, but I know both our wounds will take a while to heal. If it takes spreading her ashes over the place we call ours, if it takes burying my family in the dirt of our spot, then I'll give that to us. "Okay," I rumble. "When?"

"How about now?"

I look up at the sky to check the weather and find nothing but white and puffy clouds and a sun that shines brilliantly over a state that's seen record rain. Fitting, I suppose, that now that the town's darkness is gone, so is the bad weather. "Sure," I answer.

I move to go back around the car and hop into the driver's side, but she stops me with a hand on my elbow. I pause in my step, and with a quick look over my shoulder, I take in her pinched expression. It's enough to make me turn toward her.

I know exactly what she needs. I can read that expression better than my own these days.

Taking the urn, I set it on the roof of the car and then gather her in my arms. I snake a hand up her back, tangle my fingers in her hair, and tip her head so that I can capture her mouth properly.

The kiss is slow and reassuring, exactly what she needs, and she responds in the same way, sighing contentedly into my mouth. Even though she's emotionally damaged right now, I do find my own sort of comfort in moments like these. I almost let her die to save her, almost took her from my life so she didn't live the unthinkable things for the rest of hers. Would I do it again? Yes. But that doesn't mean I don't still feel the moment of loss I felt in that basement. It doesn't mean it doesn't creep into my thoughts, a constant reminder that the Lillian almost took everything from me again.

So I linger in the kiss, letting her direct it in any way she needs. Her fingers snake under my jacket then under my shirt, and they clutch the muscles along my back. She holds on as she takes what she needs from me, and when she's finally had her fill, she pulls away from me.

Lips swollen, foreheads touching, she whispers, "Say it again."

I smile a little. "I love you, Tori. I'm not going anywhere."

And I mean every damn word.

Chapter 36

Dear Reader…

LET'S look into the future.

I HOPE you enjoyed the Bouquet of Lies Duet. This duet holds a special place in my heart, and I hope it found room in yours too. It helped me work through my own fears, and I don't know if it helped you through yours or if it gave you new ones. Either way, I hope you enjoyed the lives of these four special characters.

I like to think that Tegan and Cole had a baby girl named after Cole's sister. After all, they visit her grave often, making sure she's not alone even in death. What better way to honor someone they love than to let her live on through their child?

They had more children, a boy and a set of twins. After the first baby, however, Cole found his inner father, and Tegan enjoyed watching him play with their kids on the front porch with a mug of coffee. Always coffee, in hopes that she'd be able to keep up with all their antics. They're a rowdy bunch, but she wouldn't have it any other way.

Cole continues to work for Derek and has taken on the role of his sole handyman for each and every business that Derek owns. Their relationship grew into a friendship. Well… as close as a friendship as Cole would ever allow.

Tegan continues to work at Tori's shop, sometimes taking the kids with her to see their auntie. Tori never minds when the kids come along because, even though she never wants children, she finds that she enjoys Tegan's. Spoiled them even by sneaking them treats and candy and donuts whenever Tegan isn't looking.

I also like to think that Tori and Killian lived happily ever after. Marriage was never in the cards for them, and neither were kids. But they grew old together and lived a life so full of love that they didn't need those things.

Killian moved into the house when Tori came home from the hospital. She hadn't known it then, but he grabbed his things from the B&B and stuffed what little belongings he had into a section of her closet. He never left.

Although Killian's torture days are over, he did find fulfillment in actual hunting. Turkey, mostly. He found that they annoyed him most, and they tasted better than deer. Along with that, he used some of the money he had to buy a few cabins in the woods. He rents them out every weekend, even in the winter, as hunters come from all over at any time of the year.

Although Killian and Tori have sworn off children, they did rescue a dog. They named this black labrador Bruce, and Tori started a social media account for him that became popular quickly when she started dressing him up in costumes that were sown by Susan in Derek's new business. Those costumes are now sold at her Wiccan store, and they can barely keep them on the shelves.

Pierce and Susan raised the Lillian's child as their own and eventually got married themselves. Although Pierce was a ripe prick, he became Susan's rock, and they're inseparable. He became exactly what she needed and the man he was always meant to be.

Pastor Kent died in prison. It turns out that even the worst criminals don't all agree with what he had done, and when Kent tried to pull his mighty and righteous behaviors in the courtyard, he was shanked by a sharpened toothbrush. So sad. Let's all take a moment to grieve.

Josiah's father is in a full security loony home. In court, he pleaded insanity and won, and it is everyone's hope that he remains crazy for the rest of his life and never has the sun beat down on his face again. He spends his nights crying for the loss of his child and his days so high on drugs that he drools. Again, let's take a moment to grieve.

Fairview went on as normal after the Lillian died. No other major event happened in that pocket of Utah, and the events of the last year only brought the people closer together.

That is all. I hope I gave you some peace knowing that your favorite characters lived the life they deserved.

- DV Fischer

About the Author

USA TODAY Bestselling author DV Fischer is a mother of two very busy boys, a wife to a wonderful husband, an owner of three sock-loving German shorthairs, and slave to one rescued cat. Together, they live in Sheldon, Iowa.

When DV Fischer isn't chasing after her children, she spends her time typing like a madwoman while consuming vast amounts of caffeine. Known for her wide imagination, she enjoys freeing her creativity through romance that may or may not exist, no matter how much we wish otherwise.

Follow DV Fischer on Facebook, Instagram, Amazon, Tiktok, Goodreads, and Bookbub.

HEAD TO MY WEBSITE FOR OTHER BOOKS AND BOOK WARNING TRIGGERS.

Made in the USA
Columbia, SC
14 November 2024

e338ea61-376b-4384-826a-7907b067a16aR02